BLIND DATE

DEBBIE IOANNA

www.bloodhoundbooks.com

Print ISBN: 978-1-5040-8617-2

ALSO BY DEBBIE IOANNA

Abberton House

This book is dedicated to my very own 'girl squad' who are always there for the good, the bad, and the hilarious bits in the middle xxx

CHAPTER 1

$\mathcal{I}$ stared at the menu before me, purposely hiding my face from the man sitting in the chair opposite. My date. I can't remember a time when I felt less inspired, by both a menu and another human being. Although if I had to compare, the prospects of food poisoning from 'Gino's Chicken Surprise' did seem a tad more exciting than my current situation. The fact that he brought me somewhere that was located above an Indian takeaway, next door to a nightclub and in the centre of Bradford should have been a huge indication that this was *not* going to be a match made in heaven.

"He's in education," my best friend Sarah had told me the week before over drinks. *"He is very well respected and very well paid* (she winked)*, you need to meet him. I'll give him your number and make sure he calls you!"*

Sarah could have omitted the part about him being in education, because he had the look of a teacher. Not the fun colourful kind you might get in a primary school, but the stuffy one in a secondary school. Someone who is full of knowledge and extremely intelligent but has no ability to teach and so waffles on about photosynthesis, not knowing that he has no control of his classroom.

His tweed jacket with a matching waistcoat suggested he had not changed his clothes between finishing work and meeting me. The mustard stain on his sleeve confirmed it. I now had a fair amount of doubt that Sarah knew this man well at all. He could very well be her neighbour's cousin's stepbrother's dentist's friend that she happened to meet for five minutes and thought would be a good match because we're similar age and single. Although judging by his attire and handlebar moustache, he could have been in his fifties.

Sarah had a knack for talking me into situations I would later regret. Back in our teenage years, she convinced me that a holiday to Zante would be great for a quiet girls' holiday with a few evening cocktails and sunbathing by the pool. That was a hard lesson learned... However, at thirty years old I didn't like the idea of a blind date she was suggesting. Having to make such an effort for a stranger on a Saturday night when I could be at home watching the latest episode of Sherlock with a Chinese takeaway seemed far too unnecessary. Surely, I'm too old for this?

I must admit that after he'd called, I'd been intrigued by Gerard's husky voice and desire to meet me so soon. Maybe Sarah had over exaggerated to him my "beauty" like she had told me about how "interesting and exciting" this man was. "She has these wonderful laughter lines; our Jenny has an infectious smile!" I can hear her saying to him about the wrinkles that were creeping up on the sides of my mouth. "Her long flowing locks glisten and shine so fabulously in the sun, it's gorgeous!"

Hopefully she's not referring to the rogue strand of grey hair which I always notice by chance as it catches the light as I walk past a mirror, but then can never actually find on purpose to yank out of my head. I can honestly say that the most interesting thing this man had said to me thus far tonight in his "husky" voice was that he should avoid eating anything too thick and fatty as he has a lot of phlegm sitting in his throat and he would hate to cough it over me. Nicholas Sparks could use some of his lines as inspiration for his next romance novel.

"Yes, that's the thing about teaching," he began. Were we talking about teaching? I hadn't noticed. "You can see the children absorbing the information as you give it to them."

"Oh, yes?" Children? He must be a primary school teacher then. "What age group do you teach?"

"Fifth form." Fifth form, what's that? Does he mean sixth form? Or is that an old term for year eleven? "So, I'm getting them ready for their science GCSEs. Very, very fascinating stuff. Did you enjoy science at school?"

"I never really understood most of it." It was my least favourite subject and I slacked off, hence my terrible grade.

"Which part did you struggle the most with?" His gaze made me uneasy, like I was in detention.

"Erm, I never really got the whole periodic table and how they wanted us to memorise it. Surely that's impossible."

"Well!" He clapped his hands, frightening the waiter who almost dropped a tray of cutlery. Gerard didn't notice. "I have the perfect solution, there's a song. It goes like this..." he coughed to clear some of that phlegm in his throat, not covering his mouth in the process. *"There's Hydrogen and Helium..."*

And just like that, he was lost in song. Luckily, this almost-empty restaurant meant I didn't have many people around me to witness my humiliation. I had never been to Gino's. I'd never even heard of it before Gerard had booked it. The menu options were cheap so I wasn't convinced of Gerard's supposed wealth if this was where he'd wanted to take me for a first date. *"Copper, Zinc and Gallium..."* I should have turned round before we'd been led to our sticky table. I noticed the walls were an unintentional yellow with questionable green stains. Cobwebs plagued every corner. There was a lingering smell of over-used oil too. The Asian waiter handed me the menu of the Italian food while I spied a Chinese chef walking out of the customer toilets with a finger in his ear. Always a good sign. At least Dean Martin was singing "That's Amore" in the background to add some authenticity to our "Italian fine dining" experience.

"Tennessine and Oganesson, and then we're done!"

Once Gerard had finished his operatic attempt at the periodic table song, the waiter finally deemed it safe to approach and take our orders. I'd decided on tomato soup with a bread roll, what could go wrong with this? Once Gerard had established with the waiter, who had limited English, that the lasagne wouldn't contain mushrooms, would have extra garlic, grated cheese rather than sprinkled (this was very important), peppers chopped up too small to see but large enough to taste and be served with a side salad of just cucumber without the skin, we could proceed with our date.

Forty-seven minutes later, not that I'd been clock watching, we had consumed our food. I had finished my gloopy red water they labelled soup and Gerard had fully dissected his lasagne for signs of mushrooms before reconstructing it to eat it. Conversation had been fast flowing for quite some time. Fortunately, it was not between Gerard and me but instead Gerard and another waiter named Israr. They had discussed in detail Israr's life and why he had come to this country (he was born in England), why he had started working in such a respected profession (he was a full-time student and worked here to help support his family) and what his hopes and dreams were. I don't think they would have noticed if I'd left. They seemed quite content with each other's company, which suited me nicely.

"Well then, Jenny!" Gerard said with far too much energy. He startled me as I'd been wondering what Benedict Cumberbatch had been doing in this week's episode of Sherlock. I hope it recorded. The bill had arrived at our table and Gerard had been studying it very hard. Presumably making sure that his discount was applied for leaving mushrooms out of his food before paying it in full. "Your share is £12.98 exactly, do you have the cash?"

I hate Sarah.

CHAPTER 2

$\mathcal{S}$undays are meant for lazing around in oversized pyjamas with unwashed hair and the smell of the previous night's Chinese takeaway on your skin, occasionally finding the odd bit of rice in your cleavage (is that just me?). I love nothing more than being reminded that I have leftover chow mein and spring rolls waiting for me in the fridge to scoff with my morning cuppa. This Sunday however, I had to go and meet Sarah for lunch and kill her for thinking I could possibly want to go on a date with Gerard. I wouldn't necessarily kill her, of course, but I would be making her pay for lunch. I would be having steak. Large. With all the trimmings. Extra fries. And a bottle of Merlot. The expensive one.

I had a few things on my to-do list. First, I would need to trawl through all my cupboards to find some Imodium to help my insides recover from the previous night's "fine dining" with Gerard. Who would've thought something as simple as tomato soup could make you feel queasy? I needed to clean out the cat litter too as the smell was taking over the landing. I would also make sure the cat was still alive. I'd not seen him for a couple of days now I thought about it. He's usually hard to miss. I should call my mother so she knew *I* was still alive. Last thing on the list: Kill Sarah.

As I climbed out of bed to make my way to the bathroom, I was suddenly met with the pain that could only come from standing on a cat's tail. I'm not sure who screamed the loudest, me or Bing Clawsby, but I definitely came off worse as now I had a whopping great scratch down my calf. At least I know the cat was still alive, so that was one thing off the list. As for his cat litter, he can wait another day after that violent reaction. It was his own fault anyway for sleeping on the floor next to my bed.

Once I'd managed to find a suitable plaster to cover the claw mark on my leg, I made my way downstairs into the kitchen. Bing, or rather Freddy Krueger, was waiting for me on the kitchen counter, butt-kissing my new scarf from Joules which I'd thrown on there the previous night in frustration after a wasted evening. I wouldn't normally wear a scarf in late June but there had been an unseasonable chill in the air. It is a British summer after all.

"If you're wanting breakfast you can wait," I said. "I need a cuppa first." I'm not sure why people talk to cats, they never respond, but they definitely understand. If looks could kill then Bing would have killed me long ago. While I was pondering whether to have toast or crumpets, I got a text from Sarah checking we were still meeting for lunch.

Yes, I reply. *I need to give you all the "juicy" gossip from last night... ahem.* I throw in an angry-face emoji for good measure.

> Oh no, that doesn't sound good! I'll wear my
> body armour ;) See you at La Luna! X

Sarah and I love going to La Luna. It's right in the centre of Halifax and by far the best Italian restaurant around without visiting Italy itself. If you want a mundane pizza or sloppy pasta dish, then go to Frankie and Benny's. If you want proper, authentic, decent Italian food then get to La Luna.

With my phone in hand I made a hasty call to my mother to let her know: I'm still alive, I'm still single, no I'm not freezing my eggs, no I'm not joining any dating sites, yes, I'm eating healthily (occasionally, sometimes… there was that tomato last week), I'm definitely not freezing my eggs, yes I'm using the anti-wrinkle cream she sent me (the tub is great to lean my phone up against when I'm watching Netflix in the bath), and no, I do *not* want to hear all about my brother William and his wife expecting their third perfect child. Goodbye, Mother, I have to go and meet Sarah.

Another chore done with. Time to take care of the last item on my list.

"You are dead." I walked in the door of the restaurant and possibly terrified one of the waitresses until she realised I was aiming my threats towards the beautiful blonde sitting at the table behind her.

"That could be why you're still single," Sarah replied. "You have no people skills!" She came towards me for a hug, the iceberg-sized diamond on her left hand glistened in the sun shining through the window and reflected onto the wall. If she was to point it in the right direction I'm pretty sure she could take down a plane.

We pulled back from our hug and I sat on the chair opposite hers, sulkily dropping my bag on the floor. "Please don't set me up again. Ever. There's no point. Anyway, you got the last decent man out there."

"Oh, hush now!" She lifted the bottle of red wine and began to fill my glass. "Look, there's twelve months until the wedding. We have twelve months to find you a date. We *will* find you a date this summer."

"I'm not that arsed anymore. I've been on enough bad dates to put me off for life. Can't I just go on my own?"

"No, I'll find you someone. You wait and see." She winked as the bottle clinked back down onto the table. "You know, there is one person you could ask out. Just saying."

"Who?" I picked up my glass and took a large gulp of wine. Oh, I needed that. I had to refrain from downing it in one or else I wouldn't be able to read the menu. She wasn't answering my question. "Who could I ask out?"

"A certain mysterious man who turns you from my straight talking, confident friend to jelly on a plate? Wibble wobble, wibble wobble, *Jenny* on a plate?"

Zack. Oh, Zack. Even the thought of him makes my mouth go dry, my insides drop and my tingly area go all tingly. I've not seen him for a month, but I can picture him as though he was standing right in front of me. His black hair was messily perfect, green eyes that could melt all the ice at the North Pole, lips that I wanted to touch and such large manly hands. We work for the same company, but in different departments, so I don't see him all the time. He only occasionally greets us with his presence when he needs to be in our area. I never know he's coming until he shows up, all six foot two of him.

"You're blushing thinking about him!"

"That's the wine, I drank it too quickly." I tried to defend my rosy cheeks but I could feel the heat rising in them, almost burning me. "Oh, shut up. You know what he does to me. I can't help it." I try covering my cheeks with my hands. They give me away every time.

"Why don't you ask him out? I'll bet he likes you. How can he not?"

"If a man likes a woman then he makes a move. Do you not remember *He's Just Not That Into You*? Besides, there's no way I'm his type. He's all perfect, God-like, perfection and I'm the crazy cat lady."

"You only have one cat, and you hate him." Bing Clawsby loves Sarah, he loves everyone apart from me. "You need to stop putting yourself down. You're beautiful and fabulous. You can have anyone you want. Anyway, I keep telling you, if you get on one of those dating apps…"

"You can cut that out straight away. We've talked about this before. You somehow managed to talk me into going on blind dates, but I'm NOT joining any dating apps or websites."

"I'm not saying you'll find the man of your dreams on there, but at least have a little fun. Build up your confidence. Someone at work uses that new app, Find Me A Date. It's supposed to be—"

"Hush!" I picked up my menu. "You're putting me off my free meal."

She might set me up with strange men, but Sarah's a great friend. Ever since meeting her at our first week at university she's always had my back. But now she's getting married and potentially moving away soon after the wedding.

I knew the only reason she was obsessed with finding me someone was so I wouldn't be alone if she *did* have to move, but I honestly didn't mind anymore. Finding a man was proving to be too much hassle. I could just get a dog. They're loyal enough to love me and it'll piss Bing off too. Two birds with one stone.

Sarah picked up her menu. "Right then, which of these extortionate steaks will you be ordering to punish me this time?"

CHAPTER 3

Several hours and too many glasses of wine later, we had discussed wedding plans, possible hen do ideas and the upcoming engagement party the next weekend. Sarah also tried to broach the subject of the dating apps again. You've got to give her credit for trying.

"Look, sign up and create a profile. You don't have to meet up with anyone. Talk. Banter. Have a laugh." She reached for my phone and grabbed it before I could snatch it back. "Just let me download it and you can check it out properly tonight when you're at home."

"Drop the phone, I can't do it. My mum's been on at me for years to join up to these types of things, she even offered to pay for them. She'd sell me off to the highest bidder if she could. If she found out I had signed up she would be so smug that she won that argument."

"Since when do you tell your mum anything about your love life? Don't tell her. She doesn't have to know. It's just between us. Please?"

Sarah's big blue eyes worked their magic. I could never disagree with her for long once she gave me that look. Especially not after this much wine anyway. That was how she talked me into getting blonde highlights put in my very naturally dark hair in our first year at university. I have made sure there is no photo evidence left of that disaster. I'm so glad I lived my teenage years before smartphones, easily accessible cameras and social media became a thing.

I put my foot down. "Okay, fine, but I'm creating the profile and choosing the photo."

"Woo! That's fine! Let me see you download it though so I know you've done it. And I want screenshots tonight showing me your profile."

"Okay, okay! I will. But I need a dessert first."

❧

Once Sarah was satisfied that the app had been downloaded and I was satisfied that I'd eaten enough tiramisu, we said our goodbyes and I went to find a taxi. I wouldn't normally leave my car at home for a lunch date, but I knew there would be a lot of wine involved, so I had to be sensible. Lunch with Sarah always included alcohol. In fact, knowing us, breakfast would probably include a cocktail. A breakfast-themed one though, perhaps. With a slice of orange or banana in there. We're not *that* out of control.

As I walked through Halifax, treading carefully on the cobbles which were clearly put there to catch out the afternoon drinkers, I suddenly realised I had some food lodged in my back teeth. Probably some of my steak. I could have left it until I got home. I could have left it until I was in the taxi. But this version of Jenny, after two large glasses of wine, was determined to free the heavenly steak from its dental grasp. I didn't want to stick my fingers in my mouth to free it though, not in public, so I used my tongue to fish around when…

"Jenny?"

I looked up, my cheek bulging from where my tongue was pushing its way to the back of my mouth and almost losing my balance on a loose cobble. Oh no, surely this was a drunken illusion? A mirage? It was him.

"Zack!" Oh, the tingles, right on cue. Why him? Why here? Why now of all times that I'm rather tipsy and elegantly getting food out of my teeth do I have to bump into him? "Hi! How are you? What are you doing here?" *All right, Spanish Inquisition, calm yourself.*

"Erm, I'm okay." He looked into my eyes, if he could read my thoughts he'd run away scared. "Are you okay? You seem a little off balance." He was looking down at my feet which were crossed over as I'd almost fallen when turning to look at him. I can't let him know I'm almost drunk on a Sunday afternoon... What would he think of me?

"I'm fine, I'm fine, I need to pee that's all." Need to pee? Need to pee?! Where's a sinkhole when you need one? I could feel the heat rising in my cheeks again, I hated blushing in front of him. "I mean, erm..." There was no way to recover. What an idiot. "Yes. I'm fine."

"Okay." He laughed. With me? *At* me? Who could tell at that point. "Listen, I'm working from your office tomorrow, so I'll probably see you in the morning."

"Oh, great stuff. I'll fill the kettle for you, ha-ha." *Fill the kettle? Seriously? I should film some of these meetings to show my mother so she stops asking me why I'm still single.*

"That's good to know." He looked at his watch. I'd be in a rush to leave me as well. "I have to go, see you in the morning."

"Yeah, bye." I watched him walk away, not able to take my eyes off him.

What is it with me when I'm near him? Some kind of force takes over me turning me into a stuttering, embarrassing mess of a woman. I can't control my words, I can't control my stance and quite frankly I act like a moron. I hope he didn't see any food in my teeth. I dug in my bag for my mirror to check my teeth and quickly wish I hadn't. Had I not opened up that compact then I would have gone home and managed to salvage the rest of my Sunday regardless of that embarrassing meeting, but no, I had to look. I had to look at myself in the mirror and spot the cream from the tiramisu which was on my chin and down my jumper. What a tit.

※

By the evening I'd managed to sober up completely, which meant I couldn't stop reliving my encounter with Zack over and over. I was thinking about it that much that all the frowning was giving me a headache.

My phone buzzed.

Have you done your profile yet? Get on it! X

Sarah wouldn't stop pestering me until I sent her evidence of my completed profile. Unfortunately, I hadn't done it yet.

Doing it now, I quickly typed. *Bear with me Xx*

For God's sake. Here we go.

I clicked open the app that Sarah had downloaded earlier and started looking through the profile and what information it wanted from me. There was basic stuff: name, age, location. It reminded me of the MSN chat room days where you'd be constantly asked "ASL". Today's kids wouldn't have a clue what that meant which was very sad.

I had to tell it if I was looking for a man or a woman (or if I preferred not to say as I was gender neutral). It wanted to know what I liked to do in my free time, my ideal date location, if I wanted someone who was teetotal or enjoyed drinking, if I was looking for someone of a particular religion, favourite movies, favourite music, favourite holiday destination. It went on and on.

Once I'd finished, I felt like I'd just written my own autobiography.

Now for the photo. The guidelines suggested a recent photo to give any potential dates a realistic image of who they're chatting to. Luckily, I had a nice photo of myself from my cousin's wedding a year earlier. That would be recent enough, right?

Okay, now to upload my completed profile.

I promptly sent Sarah a screenshot of my profile page so she knew I'd done my assignment.

> Well done! Love that photo of you, you'll get loads of dates! Let me know when someone messages you! X

It was really late by the time I was finished so I decided to go to bed. It had worked though, I had completely forgotten about how much I had embarrassed myself in front of Zack earlier and that I would be seeing him first thing in the morning... dammit.

CHAPTER 4

I decided the best way to salvage my embarrassing encounter with Zack was to wake up extra early so I could get showered and wash my hair so I could try to make myself look fabulous. Well, as fabulous as one could manage in a dull, navy work uniform. Then I would make sure I arrived at the office early so I could sit at a desk which would be as far away from Zack as possible and avoid him all day. That was the plan...

I somehow managed to sleep through my alarm and ended up rushing to get dressed and was left with little time to try to make myself look decent. Bing glared at me from the corner of my room. He was smiling at my panic, I could tell. My hair decided it didn't want to co-operate but luckily my eyeliner went on perfectly (on fleek, is that what the kids say these days?) so at least my face looks presentable. Although I needed some concealer for under my eyes. I was not happy when I pulled on my favourite trousers to discover they were a bit tight. That tumble drier keeps shrinking my clothes. What a naughty machine...

I'm not as thin as I used to be. The "gym freak" days of my early twenties are long behind me and I much prefer to chill after work with a takeaway than burn off the extra calories consumed. Whenever I drive through Halifax and pass the gym on a Friday night, I see people running on the treadmills in the windows and can't help but wonder... what *are* you doing? Life's too short to be worried about being a size eight. If you're training for a marathon then fair enough. I can't believe there are people who choose to go to the gym *before* work. I mean, seriously, have a word with yourself.

Miraculously, I found a parking space quite close to the office building. I didn't have time to grab a coffee from the Costa next door, so I'd have to risk bumping into Zack in the staff kitchen. I could smell the caffeine and croissants as I walked past their door. *"I'll fill the kettle for you"*. Oh, I cringed as I recalled how stupid I sounded the previous day. I would have to try to sound more intellectual today.

As easily as I somehow manage to embarrass myself in front of Zack, we do have some good banter together. When *Game of Thrones* was on, we'd spend ages talking about that. Same with *The Walking Dead* and now *Stranger Things*. No one else in the office watches it, but he and I have the same understanding that it is one of the greatest shows ever created, and so manage to discuss our thoughts and predictions on where the series is going to go. It was a great excuse to have a one-on-one conversation with him, and I took full advantage of it. Unfortunately, the new season was not due out until the following year so that topic would have to wait.

I walked through the office doors that, even though labelled "automatic" still required me to press the "open" button. To me, that isn't automatic, that requires manual labour and is another example of how I can make a tit out of myself with very little effort. My first time coming here I stood in front of the door waiting for it to open, but nothing happened. I stepped forward, back and then forward again, to the side, a little hop, but nothing until some highly amused person on the other side decided to point to the button for me.

I'm now trained in the use of the not-automatic door though, so this morning I glided in quite nicely and hastily made my way in the direction of the kitchen.

"Morning, Jenny!" my manager called out from her desk, a bit too loudly.

"Morning, Angela."

A few faces looked up from their desks and said hello. I noticed then that all the good desks were taken. There was only one desk free for me, and who should happen to be sat next to it?

Dammit. It was all I ever wanted at work but also my worst nightmare rolled into one. I'd be sat next to him all day. All day! I was going to need something other than *Stranger Things* to talk about. The weather? Current affairs? Maybe not...

I quickly sent a text to Sarah as soon as I made it to the kitchen.

> It's finally happening, I'm having a nervous breakdown! Xx

I filled the kettle, as I'd stupidly promised, while waiting for a reply.

> What's Bing done now? X

The last time I sent Sarah this kind of message, Bing had found his way into my sock draw and gone to battle with every single pair of tights I owned. That was not a good leg season.

> Not Bing. Sod Bing. I got to work late and the only desk free is next to him...

If it were possible to have telepathy, then I'd have been hearing her scream right then.

Flirt that arse off! Drop your pen on purpose so he has to pick it up. Undo your top button. Offer him a coffee! X

You sound like my mother! I have to go. I'll ring you tonight...X

I threw my phone into my bag and found my cup in the back of the cupboard. Should I have gone to my desk first and offered to make him a drink? Or would that have been trying too hard? I often wondered if he knew I fancied the pants off him. Surely someone that good looking knows that everyone fancies him. I hoped he didn't know how I felt, that would make things awkward.

As much as Sarah was trying to make me feel good the previous day, I firmly believe that if a man fancies you then he would make the first move. Zack and I have known each other for some time, we're the same age, the youngest people in this office. Even though we didn't work alongside each other very often, he'd never remotely hinted at being interested, so I had accepted that was that. He might even be in an established relationship. We've never had in-depth conversations about our personal lives so I wouldn't know. However, it didn't mean I couldn't fantasize once in a while. He often appeared in my dreams too, and they could get rather steamy at times.

While walking to my desk, my legs began to shake. My tea was almost splashing over the sides. I managed to make it to my desk without spilling a drop which was a miracle as my hands were trembling. I had to play it cool. He was deeply concentrating on a document.

"Good morning." I managed to get my words out quite casually.

He hadn't noticed me before then. He looked up and instantly smiled. It was a good thing my cup was safely down on the desk by that point or else I would certainly have dropped it.

"Hello again," he said. "Have you recovered today?"

"Recovered?" What did he mean?

"You seemed a bit worse for wear yesterday, a tad tipsy maybe." He had a cheeky smile.

"Oh, right, yes. I might have had a few glasses of wine with my bestie, she owed me for the night before."

"What happened the night before?" He put down the piece of paper and slowly spun round in his swivel chair to face me. I wanted to climb on his lap and dry hump him.

But, oh no, now I'd have to relay my dating disaster to someone who probably has hordes of beautiful women to pick from. Now he'd know that my love life is virtually non-existent and how pathetic I am. I'm a spinster in the making. Thirty and single. An old maid. I need to be sent on blind dates because no one wants to voluntarily go on a date if they know it's with me.

"There was an incident with a blind date," I began as I logged on to my computer, I couldn't say those words while looking at him. "My friend set me up with someone who was less interesting than a cabbage."

He laughed. This was good. I loved it when he laughed, it instantly made me smile and it meant I was funny enough to be able to bring this beautiful sound out of him. Unless he was laughing *at* me, and my disaster date, and how pathetic I was because I was set up on a blind date.

"I've never heard someone be compared to a cabbage before. So, no second date then?"

"Erm, no. Definitely not." At that moment, I got a whiff of his aftershave. He smelled wonderful. I had thoughts of attacking the Boots aftershave section on my lunch break to buy it to spray on my pillow. "She's insisting on sending me on blind dates, but they're always a disaster."

"So why do you go on them then?"

Because I'm a pathetic singleton.

"Why not? You never know, one day I might actually get set up with a cauliflower and be able to have a decent conversation."

"Ha! I wish you luck." Translation: your problem, not mine.

The day went surprisingly quickly. Conversation was easy with Zack however we both had a very busy day. As a customer advisor for the local authority, my job is customer facing, and Mondays are always full on in this office with members of the public swarming my desk to moan at me about one thing or another. Streetlights were out, pavements were loose and dangerous, parking fines wrongfully issued. By five I was ready for home. I didn't know when I'd see Zack again.

"Right then." He switched off his computer after a seemingly stress-free day for himself. His specialist role meant he didn't need to see customers like I did. "That's me done. I'll see you later."

"Yes, see you later." I smiled up at him, but he wasn't looking my way. He'd already picked up his bag and was setting off towards the exit.

CHAPTER 5

I phoned Sarah as soon as I got home to relay the whole day to her. She kept looking for hints of Zack being attracted to me, but I had to shoot her down each time. Very rarely I did wonder if he had any kind of feelings for me. Sometimes it did seem like he was flirting with me, but maybe that was his way of being polite.

Just because someone was able to joke with me it didn't mean they fancied me. He was never nervous like me, he never blushed or stumbled over his words like I do. We're not even connected on Facebook, so I don't know anything about him really. I don't know where he lives, who he hangs out with, what he does in his free time. Not a clue. He could be a Mormon with five wives and twenty children for all I know.

Sarah asked how things were going with the dating app, but I hadn't even checked it since the previous night, so I promised to have a look once I hung up. Which I didn't.

Bing had been a good boy. He'd rid the house of an uninvited monster-sized spider. Sadly though, he had *not* disposed of the corpse. It was in front of my bedroom door, curled up the size of a golf ball. If I didn't know any better, I would say he'd placed it there on purpose because he knows it would freak me out and I wouldn't be able to sleep all night for fear that it was not really dead and would come back to life and attack me in my sleep.

It was nothing that the Dyson V6 couldn't take care of though. I switched it on, hovered over the corpse and with a thud, it was settled amongst the dust and crumbs of the hoover. If it wasn't dead before, it certainly was then.

I've had Bing Clawsby for four years. He's a rescue cat. As soon as I bought the house, I'd mentioned to my brother that I wanted a cat. I don't have enough time for a dog, but cats are low maintenance and take care of themselves. Plus, kittens are super funny and cute. But big bro and his wife Liz told me to rescue one from the RSPCA. *"There are so many loveable cats out there needing homes, why buy a kitten when you can rescue one?"*

Eventually they talked me into it, convincing me that I'd be doing a good deed. Why would I want to buy a cute kitten that would grow to love me when I could adopt an adult cat that already hates me? What chance did I have with a man if I couldn't convince a cat that I was not the enemy? I give him food, shelter, toys, what more could he want?

When I saw him in his cage at the rescue centre that Christmas, I fell in love. He was an all-white winter wonderland cat with bright blue eyes. That was where the name came from, a "White Christmas" cat… So beautiful, so angelic, and so deceptive. One week into our relationship he had climbed into my Michael Kors bag and eaten the lining. One month into our relationship he weed in my knicker drawer. When I was a child, I remember we had a cat that went out one day and never returned, I was heartbroken. I try to let Bing out every day… but he always returns. Go figure.

No matter how much we seem to dislike each other, he mostly sleeps on my bed with me. I don't know if that's because he secretly loves and respects me or knows how awkward it is for me to move my feet with him in-between them. Either way, I don't mind him there. He's company after all.

I heard my phone buzzing on the kitchen counter. It was a text from Sarah.

> I've found you the PERFECT guy! Max's cousin. A financial advisor. He's from Newcastle but lives near Ilkley now. He'll be at the party on Sat – see you there! Wear the red dress! X

Another blind date. What will this guy be like? At least he's related to Max, so Sarah has actually met him and the chances are he's a normal human being. Ilkley's a posh area, perhaps this one is rich and won't expect me to go halves? I'm all for paying for a meal out if it's my turn or if I've suggested the outing, but don't pull out your calculator and ask me to pay for my share. That's just bad manners.

I saved the job of checking out the dating app until I was in bed. I could have a flick through the guys on there and see what was on offer. I wonder if it's like Amazon where you scroll and scroll until you find the item you want.

I put my glass of water on the bedside table and climbed into bed and opened up the app. Bing promptly followed and made himself comfy on my feet.

Ping. Ping. Ping.

What's going on?

Ping. Ping. Ping. Ping. Ping.

All these notifications started taking over my phone, like those virus pop-ups on a computer that won't stop until you switch it off at the mains.

Harry liked your photo

William liked your photo

Steve liked your photo

Rafiq wants to meet

Darren liked your photo

Piotr sent a message

Sven liked your photo

Percy liked your photo

Karl sent a message

Craig sent a message

Alfie liked your photo

In total, I'd received seventeen messages, six requests to meet up and seventy-two photo likes. All in the space of a day. Do these people have nothing better to do?

Mmm, sexy lady. I big trousers, you like?

I don't even... I just... yeah, let's block Piotr.

Wow, you're well fit!!! Let's meet up, where do you live?? ;)

Goodbye, Alfie, who judging by his photo was barely even adult age.

Craig was deleted after I read the first word of his message. That was disgusting. How is some of this language not flagged by the company? Maybe this app wasn't a good idea after all.

CHAPTER 6

$\mathcal{I}$f not for a lovely man named Phil, I'd have been chucking my phone out of the window by Friday night. The dating app was becoming more stress than it was worth. Dirty, gross messages were being sent by disgusting old men every day who all seemed to think I would want to have sex with them because they called me "sexy". I would have thought a sexy photo would have been if I was wearing a tiny bikini while laying on a beach towel covered in oil and wiping sand out of my cleavage, not when I was wearing a floral skater dress at a wedding. If I had a pound for every nude photo request I'd been sent I could have paid off my mortgage.

Phil sent me a message on Friday as I got home from work. I'd just ordered my usual Chinese takeaway when my phone pinged. I was tempted to ignore it. All week, the messages had been the same, and the people sending them were not much different either.

Hey there, I'm Phil :) how are you?

It was the first inoffensive message I'd received so I decided to entertain it. What harm could it do? I had time before my food arrived.

Hey there, Phil, I'm fantastic thank you. How are you doing?

I should probably dial down the sarcasm. He hasn't done anything offensive, yet.

That's great! I'm good thanks, so glad the weekend's here. Do you have any fun plans?

Just a party tomorrow, my best friend's engagement. How about you?

Oh, that's a shame, I was looking at your profile and would love to meet you. I was going to see if you fancied meeting for dinner. I live near Halifax too and there's an amazing Italian restaurant, La Luna, do you know it?

Wow, this guy seems almost normal. Nothing crude, nothing creepy, he's taken the time to read my profile to see what I'm like and where I live. Maybe I should check his out...

So, he's called Phil, a thirty-two-year-old from Huddersfield. A bank manager, he lives alone with his golden retriever. He drives an Audi and loves going to the Canary Islands for his holidays. It's quite a good photo too. He looks to be standing on a boat, the sun's shining on his face and he's kind of squinting but still giving a great smile. His dark hair's blowing in the wind. Okay, I can cope with this one. Much nicer than Piotr's teardrop tattoo under his left eye.

I do know La Luna, and I love it. It's my favourite place to go :) They have a great wine selection.

We should arrange to meet up another time then, if you fancy it?

Go on, live a little.

"That would be great, I'd love to." Sarah would be so proud.

Phil and I spent the whole night exchanging messages and he seemed like a genuinely nice guy. We were getting on so well. I couldn't wait to tell Sarah that her plan had worked and this nice guy was wanting to meet me. I'd wait until a date had been arranged to tell her, but that wasn't looking good. Our free evenings clashed for several weeks.

We agreed that if we couldn't arrange to meet up soon then

we'd FaceTime one night instead. Still a date but from home. How very modern of us.

CHAPTER 7

*M*y red dress was washed, ironed and ready to make me look fabulous. I was wearing my good bra to give me some cleavage. I might only be thirty, but the ladies aren't as alert as they used to be and need some encouragement these days. My little bit of extra tummy was bulging though and I didn't like it, so had to bring out the Bridget Jones knickers to tuck it in a little. I have to get on a diet at some point. If things go well with this James tonight, or possibly Phil in the near future, I have to make some improvements. If not for them, then so I feel comfortable stripping off naked in front of someone.

Bing was eyeing up the dress hanging on my wardrobe door, so I swiftly moved it inside and away from his hungry claws.

"Don't you dare, Clawsby, you're not ruining my night before it's even begun." He stared at me with his big piercing eyes as though he was thinking of a cocky comeback but he decided against it and flicked his tail up in the air and walked out of my bedroom. He would get his way later on, that I was sure of.

Sarah had told me a little more about Max's cousin and this time I was convinced she'd got it right.

"He's called James," she told me on Thursday evening when she rang. *"He was in the army until a few years ago."* I did used to have an army man obsession. *"He's athletic."* Potential for a good body. *"And he's so funny!"* I love humour.

It would be a night for heels. Not killer heels, those days are long gone, but I would need some height to help me pull off this dress. The last time I wore killer heels was for a night out in London. The first half an hour was amazing, but the last four hours were like torture. I decided there and then that comfort trumped style.

I also decided that I was getting old to think of such a thing. Once upon a time I would never have even worn a jacket on a night out but now I'm not ashamed to take a cardigan, coat and umbrella. It's definitely an age thing. For example, I used to carry my ID in case anyone asked my age when serving me alcohol. Now it's in case I needed identifying because I've drunkenly fallen into a ditch because I tripped on my ridiculously high heels.

I was being picked up by Sarah and Max to help them set up the venue for their engagement party. There would be various decorations to put up and, being the only bridesmaid, it was part of my duty to offer up some hard labour. It also gave me time to probe Max for more information on his cousin. Although he wouldn't be much help. He thought blind dates were immature and outdated.

"So, what does he look like?" I asked Sarah as I got into the car. "Is he tall, dark and handsome? Bit of a Henry Cavill or more Tom Hiddleston?"

"To be honest, I'm not that sure really…"

"What do you mean you're not sure?" I don't believe it. "Have you ever even met him?" My fantasy of a hunky army man was fast drifting away. I was now picturing an overweight dwarf.

"Not technically… I've seen photos of him," she said with a bit more enthusiasm. "But I've never met him. Don't worry, he looks like such a nice guy!"

Max was shaking his head from the driver's seat.

"When are you two going to stop this charade?" He shook his head disapprovingly.

I defended myself. "It's not me, it's her! She insists on setting me up, however this time, *she's* not met him either! He could be a freak for all she knows."

"James is not a freak," Sarah piped in. "Max, tell her he's not a freak."

"Leave me out of your plotting. I'm the groom tonight, not Cilla Black. My involvement in any kind of dating is over." He moved his hand from the steering wheel and placed it on Sarah's leg.

I suddenly regretted making such an effort with my appearance. I was having flashbacks to my date with Gerard. This would be the last time I let Sarah set me up with anyone. The last!

It didn't take us long to get the venue all ready and decorated exactly how Sarah had envisioned it. Sarah's parents were there to help, and it was soon a beautiful room. Ivory and gold balloons were floating from each table. Every table had a gold runner and the cake had its own special platform with space for cards and gifts. It was a very elegant two-tiered cake with white icing. There was a gold ribbon around each tier and a cake topper that said "Congratulations". Simple and beautiful.

Sarah's dad bought us all a drink each to kickstart the evening and soon enough, the guests started arriving. I was hoping to be able to stand with Sarah all night for protection against the mysterious James, but as it was her party, she had a duty to speak to everyone. I was anxiously waiting for James' arrival and wondering what fate had in store for me. I took sanctuary by the bar, my comfort zone, and made sure I had a glass of wine in my hand at all times. I was finishing my third glass when…

"Can I buy you another?"

I turned to see a good looking yet shortish man. Well, he was my height when I wasn't wearing heels, which was still short by my usual standards.

"Oh, no thank you." It was not often that a man approached me to buy me a drink, but I liked men to be tall. I can't help it.

"It's Jenny, isn't it? Sarah just told me where to find you, I'm James." He held out his hand to shake mine. I was a bit taken aback. This was definitely not a G.I. Joe.

"Oh yes, James." I shook his hand. "It's nice to meet you." Sarah could've sent me a text to say he was headed in my direction.

"You too." He had a lovely smile. In fact, he was actually quite good looking. "I'm not usually into shaking hands but, as this is my cousin's engagement party, all my family are over there so I thought I'd best act the gentleman in front of them." He laughed.

"Ha-ha, yes, that's a good idea."

"So, can I get you a drink?" He ran his hand through his sandy coloured hair.

"Yes, please." Why not? He was good looking and quite funny. How important was height anyway? We all shrink as we get older. "I'll have another white wine, please."

"Coming up."

He moved forward to stand next to me at the bar and ordered us both a drink. He was very different to Max to say they were related. James seemed quite posh, he wasn't from Bradford, that's for sure, and there were still hints of a Geordie twang in his voice.

"So, Sarah told me you were in the army?"

"Yes, I left a few years ago, I was an officer. Great experience and all that but, I'm glad to have left. What do you do?"

"Oh, my work is *very* exciting, I work in public services."

"That *does* sound exciting. As exciting as it was standing on guard duty for hours on end."

He drank his Coors Light and looked into my eyes. He was

really easy to talk to and kept making me laugh. We moved to a table and sat down so the height thing was no longer an issue. I wouldn't actually mind wearing flats for the rest of my life. It would be so much more comfortable. We spoke for most of the night and I started to really like him. Maybe Sarah did get it right after all.

"Listen," he said. "I feel a bit uncomfortable here because my family are all standing over there watching us."

I looked up to check and saw the eager eyes of aunts and grandmas all glaring in our direction.

"Are you free tomorrow?"

"Tomorrow?"

"I know it's Sunday and you're probably in church for Mass at 6am," he smiled, "but would you like to come to mine? No funny business," he held his hands in the air, "but I *am* known for my Sunday lunch. It's famous. I was helicoptered out of Afghanistan as part of an emergency mission because the locals were hunting me down for my Yorkshire pudding recipe, and it was endangering the entire British Army."

"That does sound very tempting." I *was* tempted. The more he spoke, the more I liked him. It wasn't quite tingle-tastic, but it was very close. "Will I become a target because I've tasted the awesomeness of your Yorkshire pudds?" My voice sounded so common compared to his.

"You'll need a disguise, and I wouldn't recommend holidaying in Afghanistan, but we'll cross that bridge when we come to it." When he smiled, I noticed he had perfect teeth. He must have had braces as a child. I never did, but my front teeth didn't start to cross over each other until I was in my late teens, so I never bothered to get them fixed. They're not *really* bad, but I can get self-conscious at times. "So, what do you say?"

"I'd love to." Sarah'll flip when she finds out, she'll be booking a double wedding.

"That's great!" He got his phone out of his pocket. "Put your number in there and I can text you my address." I entered my number and he dialled it. "Just checking in case you put a fake number in there. I don't want to be expecting you at my door and opening it up to a randomer or, God forbid, Megan Fox."

"Oh, the horror. You'd be so disappointed."

"Incredibly so."

We heard my phone ringing and he was satisfied.

"Great, you can save my number too," he said. "I'll text you later on with my address and I'll see you tomorrow."

"Do you want me to bring anything? A bottle of wine perhaps?" I hated going places empty handed, it seemed rude. Especially if someone was cooking for me.

"Don't worry about that, I have plenty of wine. Just bring yourself." He smiled. "Unless you happen to know Megan Fox?"

"No, sorry, never met her."

"Damn." He clicked his fingers, then reached to touch my hand. "Just us then."

Okay, there were some sparks as soon as he touched me, I'll admit it. Butterflies suddenly flew through my stomach and I felt my cheeks burning up.

"It's getting late so I think I'll be off. I can get things ready for tomorrow then."

I looked at the time on my phone and it was almost midnight, I couldn't believe how quick the night had gone. I needed to find Sarah and fill her in, but when I looked around the room, I saw her leaning on Max who was carefully supporting her. She was pissed. No, she was beyond pissed. She was wasted. I'd have to tell her the following night when she'd recovered. At least then I could tell her how well the date had gone. Even better gossip, hopefully.

"It's been lovely to meet you." We both stood. "I'll see you tomorrow."

"Yes, you will." He held out his hand. "It's been a pleasure."

We formally shook hands for all to see, but he winked at me

before he turned away. I heard my name being called from behind me. It was Max.

"Jenny, I've rung you a taxi if that's okay? Sarah's pretty pissed so I'm going to get her straight home. I'll give you some money for the fare."

"No, no that's fine I don't mind." I didn't live too far away so it wouldn't cost much anyway. "Just tell Sarah I'll call her tomorrow night."

"Are you sure? I feel bad, and Sarah'll kill me if she finds out I left you on your own."

"Don't worry about me, I'm a big girl. I'll go wait outside for it."

I gave him a hug and waved goodbye to the audience who had been watching mine and James' first meeting. My taxi didn't take long to turn up and before I knew it I was walking through my front door and running up the stairs to the bathroom. I should have peed before I left the venue.

I passed Bing who was sprawled out on the stairs. He was looking smug.

"What have you done?"

I didn't have time to wait for his answer, I was bursting for a wee. I pushed open the door to the bathroom but shouldn't have turned on the light. If I hadn't turned on the light, then I wouldn't have seen it. I would have been ignorant to Bing's crime and gone to bed all relaxed and happy with an empty bladder. But no, I switched on the light, and there it was. A dead mouse. Floating in the toilet. I hate my cat.

CHAPTER 8

*I*t wasn't difficult to find James' apartment building, although I had never been to this part of Ilkley before. He must be very wealthy. My experience of apartment buildings were entrance doors where the locks were broken, cigarette ends all over the ground, a communal post area with piles and piles of unopened junk mail and the unmistakable smell of urine. This place though was something else. For starters there was a doorman who was expecting me.

"Seventh floor, Miss Jenny. I'll get the elevator for you."

"Thank you," I said politely, fighting the urge to call him Geoffrey. I thought back to James and wondered how rich he could be to afford to live in a building with a doorman? A doorman that was actually well mannered and happy to be working on a Sunday? My mother would approve.

I stepped into the elevator and eagerly made my way up to James' floor, wondering what kind of life he lived. I'm not poor by any means but there's comfortable living and then there's luxury. I drive a three-year-old Citroen C1, he might drive a brand-new Audi. I own a small three-bedroomed end semi-detached, he might own several houses. I have a cat, he might have a tiger, who knows?

When I stepped out of the elevator I was met with the smell of new carpet. Everything was pristine. The pastel-painted walls were unblemished, unlike my own hallway which had traces of the arsehole cat's claws. There was not a speck of dust in sight. As well as a doorman, these people were paying for cleaners too. I'd hate to think how much it cost to buy one of these apartments... but then I was curious. As soon as I got home, I'd be checking Zoopla.

James' apartment was one of four on this floor. I quickly checked myself in my compact and then knocked on the door, expecting a butler to greet me, but it was James. He looked better proportioned than the previous night although I was wearing flat sandals.

"Hello, right on time." He stepped to one side as I walked in and took my coat. "I wasn't sure if you'd come. You might have had second thoughts this morning."

"How can I turn down the world's best Yorkshire puddings? It'd be very un-Yorkshire of me."

"That is true. Would you like a glass of wine?"

"Please." Wine would hopefully help to ease my nerves. I'm not used to afternoon first dates with a man. And lately, I'm not used to dates where I had already met the man, even if it was only the night before.

"What would you like?"

"White, please." My favourite.

"Which white would you like?"

Does it matter? There's only red, white and rosé to choose from.

"Erm..." I followed as he led me to the dining room and there was a display of various bottles on the counter. What a collection! "I'm not that fussed really, they all look good."

"I picked these out thinking they would best compliment the

food. You were drinking white last night so I left the red and rosé in the cabinet."

Cabinet? He has a wine cabinet? He actually has that many bottles of wine that he needs a wine storage unit. I've never owned a bottle of wine long enough to constitute putting it in storage. The longest I've ever stored a bottle of wine was the previous year when I had flu and couldn't drink any, so it stayed in my fridge until I was better. Usually it would have been devoured over a weekend. By "weekend" I mean opened on a Thursday night in anticipation of the weekend. One needs to prepare oneself.

"Erm, any wine is fine for me." I smiled. Until then I had always considered myself a connoisseur. Clearly, I knew nothing. Not only was this guy wealthy, more importantly, he knew wine. I was liking him more and more.

He carefully selected one of the bottles and pulled out the cork with a corkscrew. There was no screw top wine in this room, and I daresay none of this collection came from Tesco Express.

I could smell the beef cooking away nicely in the oven. I could almost taste it. He handed me a glass.

"Would you like a tour?"

"I'd love one." I thought he'd never ask. I'd been dying to have a nosy ever since I walked in. Sarah would expect a very detailed description for a perfect visual. I had always imagined apartments to be noisy with people living all around you, above and below, but it was silent.

"Good, well, this is the dining room." The table looked small in comparison to the room itself, but he explained it was an expandable table for when he hosts dinner parties. That was another good sign, he loved to cook. I hate cooking. I don't have the patience to be buying ingredients and following recipes from celebrity cookbooks. You always have to spend a ridiculous amount of money buying herbs and spices and flavourings that you've never even heard of and would never normally buy.

By the time you've finished, you've spent a small fortune and wasted several hours making one meal. Years go by and those ingredients have all gone out of date in the back of the cupboard because you've never needed to use them again. In my opinion, it was best to leave the cooking to the professionals. By professionals, I mean the chefs at Chang's Chinese Takeaway who love me so much they send me a Christmas card every year.

We were about to exit the dining room when there was a faint beeping coming from another room.

"Oh damn, the food's ready." He looked at his watch. "Please, take a seat." He walked towards the table and pulled out a chair for me to sit down. "I'll be right back with dinner and then we can resume the tour once we've finished."

"Sounds lovely," I said, suddenly feeling aware of my very Yorkshire accent next to his. I wondered if his parents were posh too. If I ever met them, I'd hope they didn't think me too common.

My desire to be nosy was suddenly taken over by my hunger pangs. I love Sunday dinner. A plate full of tender beef, perfect Yorkshire puddings and crispy roast potatoes, vegetables too. And all of it swimming in thick hot gravy almost spilling over the sides. Amazing. If I was ever on Death Row, that would be my last meal. That with a side order of fish and chips of course. My stomach suddenly made a very loud churning noise, as though telling me off for teasing it with thoughts of food. I took a sip of my wine and had to stop myself downing the whole glass. It was the nicest wine I'd ever tasted, and it tasted expensive. It was definitely not Blossom Hill.

I tried to distract my hungry belly by having a look around the room. I couldn't see the wine cabinet, but there was a beautiful unit by the wall. There was nothing on top of it. Usually people decorate units with photos, vases, tacky ornaments, but this one was bare. Maybe it was new and he'd not yet decided how to accessorise. Men aren't always too sure about buying knick-knacks.

"Here we go!"

James re-entered the room with two plates with steaming hot food on them, I couldn't wait to dig in. He placed it in front of me and I was confused. Where was all the food? I'd skipped breakfast for this. There were two very perfectly symmetrical yet very small Yorkshire puddings, three small whole carrots surrounded by twenty peas (yes, I counted), five small new potatoes which had been roasted still in their skins, and a tiny bundle of beef held together with a string. Where I come from, your plate should be overflowing with food for this kind of meal. If you were presented with this at a Toby Carvery, you'd be asking for your money back.

"Oh, almost forgot!" He jumped up from his chair and went to the unit by the wall and slid open the door. It was a hot food storage unit, now it made sense. Maybe the rest of the food was in there. Silly me.

He came back to the table with a very small jug which contained the gravy, and that was it. No trays of proper roast potatoes or mashed swede or extra Yorkshires, just gravy. He carefully dribbled a very small amount onto his Yorkshire puddings and then offered it to me.

"Thank you." I took the jug and carefully poured some onto my food, not wanting to make a mess. Growing up I'd often heard the phrase "how the other half live", I didn't know it referred to food and the lack of it.

It didn't take us long to eat our food, surprisingly. We managed to find a lot to talk about in the short space of time. I made sure to take small bites so my meal lasted longer than it probably should have done. He told me about his travels around the world while I daydreamed about Chang's and what I would be ordering tonight. Actually, so what if he served tiny portions of food? It might do wonders for weight loss. A lifetime of flat shoes as well as a potentially flat stomach? I can work with that.

We finished the bottle of wine and he opened a second.

"I'll clean up later, how about the rest of the tour?"

"That sounds great."

We left the table and walked back out into the hallway. As soon as I stood up, I felt the wine beginning to take effect. I was meant to be driving myself back home. If only I could have had a big meal to soak up the alcohol... He led me into the next room which was an office. A very tidy office. In front of one wall were two huge units packed with books. Travel books, biographies, cookbooks, fiction, history, lifestyle, the lot. It was like a miniature library.

The room next to this was the lounge. The large L-shaped sofa was facing the biggest TV I'd ever seen on the wall, and not a wire in sight. The wires surrounding my 32" TV, Sky box and DVD player are surely a hazard. There were more shelves with books. Photos of army parades and medals on the walls. The carpet looked so spongey, like every footstep would be similar to stepping into quicksand, however instead of drowning your feet you would sink into a sea of carpet.

He showed me where the bathroom was, and then the kitchen, however he didn't want to linger in there for too long as he didn't want me to see the mess from cooking. He can never come to my house if he doesn't like mess. All my clothes from the week were in a pile in front of my washing machine, the draining board was full of bowls and plates that needed putting away and I was pretty sure my bin hadn't been emptied in some time.

The last room on the tour was the bedroom. We looked in from the doorway. He had a king-sized bed with silver damask bedding with wallpaper to match. The room was perfect. The entire apartment was perfect. It was like one of those articles celebrities have in magazines to show off their perfect homes and perfect lives. I could get tips from James on how to maximise space and find wallpaper to match the bedding according to which season we were in. I then looked above my head and saw a bar across the door.

"What's this for?" I asked.

"It's a pull-up bar, so there's no excuse not to do any exercise on a morning. I get out of bed and make sure I do a few pull-ups before I'm allowed to have any breakfast. Try it."

Was he kidding? I struggle to carry shopping bags from my car, there's no way I can support my own weight. Has he seen my thighs?

I stepped back away from it. "Oh, no. I wouldn't be able to."

"Of course you can, I'll help. Put your arms on the bar." I was suddenly faced with thoughts of him in the army, giving orders. Hello tingles... I'd wondered where you'd gone.

It must have been the wine, or his beautiful smile, but I did as I was instructed and lifted my arms, grateful I'd shaved under them that morning. He put his hands on my hips and the tingling intensified. He looked into my eyes and got closer to my face, bringing his lips to mine. I brought my arms back down from the bar and put them around his neck while he kissed me. It was a good kiss. There was potential.

James led me into the bedroom and onto the bed. Clothes were removed and thrown on the floor as he laid on top of me. I'm glad I opted for the matching black lace bra and knickers. I was impressed with his skill to continue kissing me, his tongue gently teasing mine, while at the same time reaching his arm round my back to undo my bra in one, swift, very impressive motion. Even I struggle to twang it open at times.

He reached into the drawer by the bed and pulled out a condom. I didn't look while he put it on, I didn't want to put him off and ruin the moment. Also, I could be a bit of a prude when it came to looking at naked men. Sarah could never understand why, but she and Max had been together for years, she was used to seeing it wobble about but I didn't see the need. It wasn't long before James was back on top of me and ready for some afternoon delight. I was ready, the moment was now.

That's the thing about moments. They have the ability to surprise you. Have you ever been so excited about something that you couldn't wait for it to happen? The build-up of anticipation and tingles where a single touch would make you explode in a world of absolute pleasure.

This was not one of those moments.

There he was, giving it his best and evidently enjoying himself, thrusting inside me with all his might however... I couldn't feel a thing. Oh, the horror. What a waste of a notch on the bedpost. In-out, in-out, in-out. He was pushing his weight down on me that much, I couldn't even attempt to flip over to get on top. At least if I was in control I could try to salvage some of this encounter.

"Is that good?" he panted. "Do you like that?"

"Oh, yes," I managed, "mmm, yes, keep going." I'd never been a fan of faking. Why waste an opportunity for an orgasm? In this case though I'd have more luck dry humping a cloud.

And so, he went on. And on. And on. And on.

Damn, I forgot to set record for Call The Midwife *tonight. I'm sure I'll be home in time.*

And on. And on. And on.

Or maybe not. I can't remember what happened in last week's episode, I'll have to have a recap before I watch the new one.

And on. And on. And on.

I'll have to make sure I do the Tesco online shop tonight too. Running out of bread. Might get some currant tea cakes this time. Not had them for years. Ooh, love a toasted tea cake on a morning with a cuppa. Or crumpets. They'd be good too.

And on. And on. And on.

Want to try take lunches to work with me, break some bad habits of spending money when I'm there. I spend a fortune on lunches at Greggs and Subway... could save so much money making it before I go. They do some good paninis at Costa though. And with a Mocha too? Perfect combination.

"Oh, baby, that's good!" he called out.

"Oh yes," I tried to sound sincere. "Yes, keep doing that."

Donuts. I'll buy some donuts. I've had a healthy-ish week, I deserve a treat.

And on. And on. And on.

Forty-five minutes later… he called out in a way that told me he was done. I'd been flipped on my front, on my back, leg up, two legs up, every way possible. I was exhausted. What the hell was he doing that he could have lasted so bloody long? Was he secretly planning his weekly food shop too?

He laid beside me, panting with a satisfied smile on his face. He was proud of his work.

"I'll try to last longer next time, I'm not usually that quick, I'm sorry."

Quick? Is he having a laugh?

CHAPTER 9

I arrived home later that afternoon feeling sore and achy from the bedroom gymnastics and absolutely starving. James was hoping I'd stick around for pudding, but I was knackered after that performance. I told him I couldn't stay much longer as I needed to feed the cat, when really, I had sneakily ordered a Chang's from the Just Eat app on my phone when James was in the bathroom. I had an hour and fifteen minutes to get home.

I got there as my favourite delivery driver pulled up.

"Jenny, my friend." Lots of people are on first name terms with their takeaway drivers, aren't they? "Here, your food."

"Thank you, Imran."

"Early for food today, yes?"

"Yes, very hungry." I rubbed my belly in case he needed a visual to understand what the word "hungry" meant while working as a delivery driver for a fast food company.

"Okay, okay. Enjoy." He chuckled as he handed me my food and went back to his car as I fumbled for my key to get in the house.

I finally got the door open and didn't even bother to take off my coat. I grabbed a plate and fork from the kitchen and took it into the living room. I put the bag of food on the coffee table and began to open all the containers, filling my mouth with food at the same time. I couldn't help myself. There was fried rice. Noodles. Salt and pepper chicken. Salt and pepper chips. Spring rolls. Prawn crackers. I never eat the prawn crackers, they always end up in the bin, but this time they would be getting eaten.

I sat there for an hour filling my belly and watching TV. Bing came to sit with me, but only because it was time for some butt-licking cat yoga. He liked to save this party trick for when I was eating.

"Shoo, you disgusting animal." I was far too full at this point to get up and throw him out so nudged him with my foot instead. He got the message and walked out after giving me a dirty look.

Oh, that food was good, but I forgot to bring a drink to the lounge with me. I'd get one when I had the energy to move. It wasn't worth standing up yet. My phone buzzed in my pocket. It was a text from James.

I had a great time, your so sexy ;)

Oh, grammar. A pet peeve. Every time someone says "your" instead of "you're" I'm reminded of the episode of *Friends* where Ross lectures Rachel on the correct usage of the words. How come nearly every moment in life can be linked to a *Friends* reference?

Me too, that was great X

I didn't know what else to say. I didn't want to give any hint at wanting a second date. I couldn't cope with that. I've had disappointing sex before, but that was back in my teens when no one knew what they were doing. It shouldn't be happening at thirty. We've all got access to Google, Wikipedia, and even YouTube if you're that desperate and need some tips.

> We should do that again sometime, are you free next weekend?

Dammit, what now?

> No, sorry. Going away next weekend, I'll let you know when I'm free :) X

I lied.

My phone rang before I could put it down, I prayed that it wasn't James calling me to convince me to go back to his sometime soon. I checked and it was Sarah, relief.

"Jenny," this delicate voice muttered, "oh my God, my head."

"Feeling a bit rough today, my dear?" I picked up a spring roll and let the crispy outer layers crunch as my teeth sunk down into it.

"Rough. Sick. Dying. I've been in bed all day and just woke up. Max was telling me you and James were talking all night so I had to call and find out how it went. Did you hit it off? Are you going on a date? Have my cupid skills *finally* worked?"

"Funny you should mention that…"

I told her about it all – from start to finish – and that the meal was not the only disappointment of my Sunday.

"Oh no, that's awful!" It was half disappointment and half laughter in her voice.

"Yep, and now he's texting me wanting a repeat performance. What am I going to do?"

"It's not all about size you know, Jenny. You could try different positions or toys or oral…"

"No, that's something you do after years with the same guy to try to spice things up. Not with someone you just met."

"Damn. I thought he'd be perfect for you."

"We got on fine last night but we're not at all compatible. He needs someone from a different background, a bit more proper, with a tiny stomach and an even smaller vagina." I finished off the last of the spring rolls. Did I really eat all eight of them? "So, did you have a good night? I barely saw you."

"From what I remember it was really good! But the thing I discovered is when you're the bride people want to buy you drinks. I lost count of how many wines I had. Are you eating?"

"Chinese. I ordered it before I'd left James' place. That's how hungry I was."

"Oh, you poor thing! That's making *me* hungry actually. You always pick the best stuff for a takeaway. You're the takeaway queen."

"I thought you were feeling sick and dying?"

"I am but... greasy food sounds perfect. I'll talk to you later, I need to text Max downstairs to order me some food."

"Haha, you lazy sod, get out of bed! I'll speak to you later."

"Bye!"

CHAPTER 10

The next few weeks were fairly uneventful. James tried to arrange meeting up a few times but eventually got the hint and left me alone. I was still traumatised over that particular date, but at least I managed to watch *Call The Midwife* that night. Every cloud and all that. I didn't come across Zack again, so work was pretty boring without any eye candy, and Sarah was too busy with Max to be able to meet up. Phil and I tried to arrange a date again, but we struggled to find a time we were both free.

So, it was just me with Bing for company, although he eventually got sick of me and disappeared for two nights. When he returned he was sporting an unusual lump on the back of his neck. I tried to get close to have a look, but he was having none of it. I called the vets for advice and they wanted me to bring him in.

"Are you sure?" I asked. "Last time…"

"It's fine," said the receptionist with trepidation, "there are two vets available so one of them can hold Bing down and he won't be able to bite Dr Stevens again."

"Okay, if you're sure."

The vet needed to be taken to A&E for emergency care after our last visit. There would be no permanent damage but twelve stitches later he couldn't use his hand for several weeks. I'm surprised they didn't ban Bing from returning. Whenever we have had to go, which is only once a bloody year for his boosters, he creates such a drama. Other cats sit quietly in their carriers, but not Bing. It sounds like he's in line at a slaughterhouse. It's so embarrassing.

Poor Dr Stevens. He was new to the practice at the time, and very good looking. He seemed really flirty when we had first met, but not anymore. The poor guy was not happy when he saw us walk in. You could see the fear send a shiver down his entire body when he locked eyes with Bing. Bing, true to form, stared right back at him.

"Good morning, Dr Stevens." I tried to sound jovial to clear the tension in the room.

"Good morning." He stared at Bing in his carrier while standing as far away from us as possible. I plonked Bing on the table and went to open the front to get him out. "Let's wait for Dr Judge, shall we?"

"Oh, yes of course! Sorry…" The poor guy looked petrified. I could see sweat forming on his upper lip. As he pulled his hand up to wipe away the sweat I noticed the scar, it was hard to miss it.

A grey-haired head peeked around the door, it was the unmistakable Dr Judge. A large, jolly man who had a smile for everybody, even for Bing. He'd been at the practice his entire veterinary career. I remember him from my childhood whenever we had to bring our dog for his annual booster, although he had longer, wavy blond hair back then. You could tell he was never bored of his job. He loved it.

"Hellooo! Have we not started yet, Andy?"

"No, I erm, was waiting for you," Dr Stevens stuttered.

"That's okay. Hello Bing! How're you feeling today?" Dr Judge bent down to the carrier and Bing replied with an almighty howl. "Fantastic, glad to hear it. He's still got his voice, which is good. No need to check that. Do you want to try to get him out?" he asked me.

Do *I* want to go in there and get out the savage cat? Do you think there's less chance of me being bitten because he belongs to me? Out of all of us, he's more likely to try to kill me first.

"Sure, no problem." I unzipped the front very slowly, a low growl echoing from the inside. "Come on, Bing, be a good boy." *Please, oh please be good*. The front of the carrier dropped down as Bing made his way to the back of it. Luckily, it opens at both ends. I leaned over to the other side and opened that end too which resulted in Bing sitting in the middle of it. Moron cat.

Dr Judge stepped forward. "Come on now, boy, we won't be long. We need to look at that neck of yours."

He lifted it up and tilted it so the cat had no choice but to topple out and onto the table. The hair on his back stood up on its end and his tail was as fluffed up as a feather duster. There was no mistaking the sound coming from him, he was angry. I'd be hiding my shoes and handbags later as a precaution.

"Right," Dr Judge said, rolling his sleeves up, "I'll hold him down, Andy, and you can quickly look at his neck, okay?" Dr Stevens looked petrified. "I promise, he won't get you again."

Dr Judge stroked Bing very gently behind his ears eventually moving to his neck and down his back. It relaxed him a little, but not enough. Dr Judge had to act quickly. The second Bing looked up at me, Dr Judge made his move. It all happened so fast.

Dr Judge used both his arms, one pushing down on Bing's bottom and the other pushing down from his shoulders up to his head. He couldn't move, not even an inch. And boy, was he pissed off. His little paws were leaving sweat marks on the table. He sounded like something from *The Exorcist*.

"Now, look now." Dr Judge ordered. "I can feel it under my thumb."

Dr Stevens waited a second, I'm assuming to make sure Bing couldn't move, and then had a good look at his neck.

"It's just a tick," he said, sounding relieved that it could be cured there and then without the need for a return appointment. He quickly went into one of the drawers and pulled out a small silver hook contraption. He went back into Bing's neck and within seconds he pulled out this lump of a brown insect and placed it on a tissue. "It's whole, I got all of it out."

"Goodo, Andy. Jenny, do you want to get his carrier ready?"

I zipped up one of the ends and then put it in front of Bing so he could run straight back inside it. When the vet let go of him, he ran straight in and hissed at Dr Stevens who was stood at the other side in clear view. He suddenly went very pale. There were little puddles of sweat on the table which were either from Bing's paws or Dr Stevens' upper lip.

"Will I need to do anything?" I asked, trying to distract Dr Stevens before he passed out, but he didn't hear me.

"No," Dr Judge said. "He will be fine. You can buy some tick prevention treatment like shampoo or a collar but I'm not sure how he'd react to any of that given his disposition. Let's leave it for now, ey? If you notice anymore, bring him back in."

Can I not just leave him here? He was going to make me pay for this later on. *I mean, how many other animals as small as Bing require two vets to be present?*

CHAPTER 11

*B*ing got over his traumatic morning in no time. All he needed to do was leave a massive poo on my pillow and he was back to his normal self. It's probably a good thing that I never meet a man I want to bring home. Lord knows what this cat would do to scare them off forever. The last man to spend the night woke up to find his boxers had been half eaten and his shoelaces removed. I never did find them, and I never saw that guy again. Can't imagine why.

There was always one man-friend that I can rely on when I'm feeling lonely. Or, in this case, to make up for having such a bad sexual experience. Dan and I worked together years ago. We'd never been a couple, but every now and then we meet up and have some drinks and some sex with no strings attached. Everyone needs this kind of reliable friend, and I needed him.

"Hello, stranger," he said.

"Hello, you, it's been a while."

"It certainly has. How've you been?"

"Same old same old. I found a goldmine under my house last month and bought a yacht which just sits in my garden as I'm about 200 miles from the sea. How about you?"

"Can't complain."

Our initial conversations were always the same. We didn't really care about what was going on with each other. To be honest, I can't even remember where he works or what car he drives. Only that he lives less than a mile away and it won't take me long to shave my legs and get over there.

"Are you free tonight?" I asked.

"Let me check my calendar. Hmmm, I'm super busy being all super important and stuff, I don't know if you know but I'm the new American president now."

"Oh, I thought that idiot on the news looked familiar."

"Yep, that's me. But everywhere I go there's a very angry mob of people following me so... you might need to come to mine, is that okay?"

"It is, Mr President, what time would you like me?"

"Eight's fine. Do you want me to order some food in?"

It would be so easy to say yes, however, I've had a takeaway three times this week. Having a fourth would be taking the piss. Besides, I'd found some leftover salt and pepper chicken in the fridge from two days ago. That doesn't count as a fourth takeaway meal, right? "No, don't worry about food. I'll eat before I get to you."

"Brill, okay, see you soon."

I quickly got a bath running and went downstairs to the fridge to nibble on leftover food. I'm pretty sure it's safe to eat leftover Chinese food two days later. It was too nice to throw away. By seven forty-five, I was ready to go.

Dan had a bottle of wine open when I got there. He looked different to the last time I saw him. His dark hair was longer and almost reaching his eyes, and he had finally taken that earring out.

"Cheers." We clinked our glasses like we were toasting in the new year. Once we had exchanged pointless small talk and decided that white wine was the best wine, we made our way upstairs.

One hour later, I was a very satisfied woman.

"Would you like some more wine?" he asked.

"No, thanks, I'm fine."

He lifted his arm up and I moved in to snuggle in his nook. As much as I loved the sex-only part of our relationship, it was nice having someone to cuddle up to. Having his arms wrapped around me made me feel secure and being with him was so easy. It was never awkward between us. Now I could fall asleep perfectly happy and relaxed, and I did, quite quickly.

§≈

What was that popping sound? Was that me? No way. I've not farted in my sleep for years. I did have a strange pain in my tummy though, that leftover Chinese was probably not a good idea. *No, I didn't. I think Dan's asleep, his breathing's quite heavy, so he can't have heard anything. I must have dreamt it.*

Pop.

Was that me again? I think it was. Why am I farting in my sleep? Why now? I don't think Dan's asleep anymore, maybe it's him? Must be. I'll go back to sleep.

Pop.

*Holy crap, it **is** me. Not only am I farting in my sleep, I'm farting myself awake. That was unmistakably coming from my arse. What the hell? I must try to stay awake so I can hold it in. Must stay awake. Must stay...*

Pop.

For God's sake, this is getting ridiculous. Why am I so bloody bloated? And why tonight of all nights? He'll never let me come over ever again! I can't even check my phone to see what time it is as he'll know I'm awake because I keep farting myself awake. Just need to find a way to pass the time until morning then sneak myself out of the house before he notices. Now, what would pass the time? How can I make myself stay awake all night?

Pop.

I may die of embarrassment before morning.

CHAPTER 12

*P*lease *tell me it was all a dream? That I didn't spend all night trumping in Dan's bed? Otherwise, please tell me it's really early so I can sneak out before he notices me gone?* I opened my eyes and could see the light from outside, it was morning. Now to check that Dan was asleep. When I turned my head towards him, however, he wasn't there. *Where's he gone? Did I fart him out of bed? Oh, don't joke. Maybe he's in the loo.*

I quietly climbed out of bed and found my phone in my trouser pocket. It was just past nine. So much for getting up early and sneaking out. I quickly threw my clothes on and headed out to the landing. I could hear the TV on downstairs which meant Dan couldn't stand staying in bed with me and my gas. It also meant that I couldn't leave without facing him. I can't hide up here all day.

I was nervous walking down the stairs, getting closer and closer to the bottom. I need to act like nothing happened.

"Morning." I tried to sound nonchalant as I walked into the kitchen. I could smell toast and coffee which made my belly grumble. I assume that's from hunger. Surely, I'd emptied myself of any excess gasses overnight.

"Ey up, sleepyhead." He smiled. "You were practically in a coma last night." He took a big bite of his toast.

"Was I?" Please don't tell me about the farting, my face was already starting to burn.

"Yeah, so was I really but I think you dropped off first. Must have been the wine."

"Yes, must have been. Erm, I need to get off."

"Don't you want any breakfast? You usually eat me out of house and home when you're here." It was true. He usually did the works for me; eggs, bacon, toast, beans, tomatoes, homemade hash browns, the lot. He knew my appetite very well. "I've got everything out ready to start, I just didn't know what time your lazy arse was going to come down."

"No, I'm sure. I've got loads to do." I headed to the table to pick up my bag and then walked to the door. "Last night was great though, exactly what I needed."

He put down his toast and followed me to the door.

"It was great to see you, as always. Oh, and Jenny?" he said as I stepped into the garden.

"Yes?" I turned round to face him.

"I'll smell you later." He winked.

Bollocks. I gave him a quick smile but turned before he could see my face becoming beetroot. I could still hear him laughing as I got to my car. I drove away as quickly as I legally could. I can't believe that happened. Why last night of all nights when I was with someone? It couldn't have happened when I was on my own, which was every other bloody night of the year. He'd never want to see me again.

It wasn't long before I'd pulled up outside my home. I clearly drove on autopilot because I can't even remember pulling out of junctions or turning onto my road. The sound of popping was going on and on in my head and it wouldn't stop. Absolutely mortified.

I could hear my phone ringing from inside my bag. I didn't

even want to look in case it was Dan calling to take the piss. It wasn't, it was worse than that. Much worse...

"Hello, Mother."

"You don't sound happy this morning. What's the matter with you?"

"Nothing, rough night, had a dodgy takeaway." I pulled my key out of the ignition but decided to stay put so she wouldn't know I was just getting home after spending a night out. *A one-night stand won't put a ring on it, Jenny.* The last thing I needed that morning was an interrogation into my premarital antics.

"You have too many takeaways. You're not twenty anymore, Jennifer. Your metabolism isn't what it used to be. Soon you won't just be single, you'll be fat too. Then you'll never meet a man. Is that what you want?"

"Was there a particular reason why you needed to speak to me this morning, Mother?" I wasn't in the mood for her lectures. Any other day I could take it, but not after my embarrassing night. I just wanted to curl up in a ball and sulk.

"I've found you a man. He's an *artist.*" She said it in a way that suggested this was impressive. "It's Jean's son, you know her, next door's sister? You met her once when you were about eight."

"No, I don't remember."

"Yes, you do! It was 1996, you wore that blue dress to Viv and John's wedding. You remember them, John played football with your dad."

"No, I don't remember."

"Why can't you remember?"

"Because it was over twenty years ago!"

"Anyway... Viv is friends with Margaret who lives next door, so Margaret and her sister Jean were at the wedding. That's where you met her. Jean's son is single, and I'm told he's a catch. It's all been arranged. You're meeting him a week on Saturday at 11am. The Costa Coffee in Halifax, he'll be there waiting for you."

How sad has one's life become when even your own mother is setting you up with strangers...

"Hang on, how do you know I'm not seeing someone already?"

"Because I know you. By the time I was your age, I was married with two children. All you have is a demented cat."

Now, it was one thing for *me* to insult Bing, but I wasn't having anyone else call him names.

"Don't say that about Bing! He's a unique character with specific needs."

"He's the devil incarnate. Aren't you forgetting that he peed in my bag?"

Oh yes, I had forgotten. That was hilarious. I gave him a whole tin of tuna after he did that. It made my year.

"Anyway," my mother continued. "A week on Saturday. Rob will meet you there. Dress nicely. Talk about interesting things. Don't be late! And, Jenny?"

"Yes, Mother?"

"Have you heard from your brother lately? They're having a girl!" I'd never heard her sound so happy. "Finally, after two boys they're having a girl. Isn't that wonderful?"

"Amazeballs."

"Amaze-what?"

"Never mind, I have to go. Bye."

"Next Saturday!"

"I'll be there! Goodbye!"

CHAPTER 13

*T*hursday night. That was the night. The only night that Phil and I were both free, but not to go out to meet in person as he was at a hotel in Birmingham for a work thing. It would need to be a FaceTime date. The benefit was I didn't need to rush to have a shower to make sure I smelled fresh, that my armpits were shaved and that my breath didn't smell of the garlic chicken sandwich from lunchtime. But, of course, I'm a woman which means I wanted to look my absolute best.

I was so excited to finally see his face. We had been speaking almost every day that week and I really liked him. We had so much in common and every time my phone buzzed with a message from him my heart fluttered a little bit.

I rushed home from work, so I could wash, dry and straighten my hair. I made sure my make-up was perfect and practised holding my phone at different angles in different parts of the house to see which light worked better and was the most flattering. I'd kicked Bing out of the house for the evening, so he couldn't interrupt or cause me any kind of embarrassment. It would be awkward trying to look seductive with the sound of Bing's squelching as he cleansed himself.

And so, it was soon eight. I was ready. I was fabulous. I would *not* mess this up.

"Well hello!" I said as his face appeared on my screen. I gave him my best smile and was pleased when he smiled back. It was such a warm smile. He had great teeth too.

"Hey there," his face was quite close to the camera, "you look incredible."

"Thank you." I blushed slightly. "It's nice to finally see you, it's a shame we couldn't meet in person."

"I know, it really sucks. But here we are." He seemed to zoom the camera away and he was topless. I could see his bare shoulders, a tribal tattoo covering the top of one of his arms. He was quite muscly, which outweighed his tardiness at not bothering to put a T-shirt on. I could forgive that I suppose. He's away from home in some hotel, he needs to be relaxed and comfy. "So, how was your day?"

"It was good, quite quiet really which is always a nice way to end the week. How was... erm," the camera zoomed out a little more, revealing more of his flesh. "How was your day?"

"Oh, it was great, quite chilled so I hit the gym after work. I love working out, do you?"

"Erm, not really. I think if it's a hobby then great but I've never been interested in the gym. Which one... do, erm, which gym... are you naked?"

The camera had zoomed further out and there was the unmistakeable hint of a cock staring down the camera lens. Complete with testicles. The whole family.

"I am, do you like what you see?" He gave me a wink, with the eyes on his head, and angled the camera down to show me more of his manhood. I had to tilt the phone away. I can't look at a penis directly.

"I wasn't expecting to see it, I mean you. Why the hell are you naked?"

"This is a date, I'm gutted that you're fully clothed." The

camera went back to his face and he was looking quite low at his screen, as though trying to look at my cleavage.

"So, if we'd made it to a restaurant then you would have been stark bollock bloody naked then?"

"Of course not, that would have come later."

"Okay, Phil, goodbye."

"Wait, wait, I can cover it up if you're frigid."

"Ciao!" I slammed the phone a little too hard, screen down, to make sure all naked images had disappeared from my eyesight.

What the hell happened then? I don't even know what happened. How could he think that was appropriate? He seemed so nice, what went wrong? That's it. I'm deleting the app. I'm never visiting another dating app or site ever again.

CHAPTER 14

$\mathcal{U}$sually, when walking into work on a Friday, I had a spring in my step knowing that it was almost the weekend. That day, however, I would happily fast forward straight to Monday and skip the entire weekend altogether. I was still cringing from my "date" with Phil the previous night and my mother had called me every night to make sure I'd not forget to meet up with this Rob the next day, making me repeat the time and location to her.

I've not even met him yet and already I hate him, which is really unfair. He could be such a nice guy. Artists are usually quite... I've never met an "artist". I didn't think that could be a job title these days. Van Gogh was an artist. David Hockney is an artist but he's from the era where there were no computer graphics. Nowadays, people who enjoyed doing art in school usually became graphic designers or other sort of creatives. There hasn't exactly been a mad rush for a new Bob Ross style TV show.

I was having a particularly frustrating morning. Every member of the public was being difficult, one moron after another.

"But they haven't emptied my bin yet!"

"Mr Craven," I exhaled. "Like I've said several times now, bin collections are from six in the morning until four in the afternoon. It's not even twelve yet."

"But they *always* come at seven!"

"That may be, however, some things cause delays. Roadworks, traffic jams, cars blocking the road. Sometimes their route has to be changed. If they don't make it by the end of the day, then please report it to us, but I cannot ring them now when it's only halfway through their shift."

"Useless," he pushed his chair back and his feet thumped their way down the corridor to the exit as he continued shouting. "Bloody useless!"

It was like they could sense my mood and so headed straight for me to discuss their problems. And once again, my cup of tea had gone cold before I'd had a chance to drink it. Could the day get any more annoying?

Things in the staff kitchen weren't any better. The dishwasher hadn't been unloaded, the kettle was empty, and the milk had been left out to go warm. I reached into the cupboard but there were no tea bags.

"Oh, for fuck's sake!" I don't make a habit of swearing at work, but as I was alone…

"Everything okay?"

I spun round and there he was in all his glory. Black suit trousers, a crisp white shirt with the top button undone and his hair so perfectly messy. He must have been stood behind the door as I came in but I totally missed him, which is so unlike me. I can usually sense him.

"Zack, I didn't know you were here today."

I can't believe he witnessed my tantrum, I'm mortified. Please don't let me blush.

"I got here about ten minutes ago, but you seemed to be in

deep conversation with a customer arguing over bin collections. Is everything okay?" he looked deeply concerned.

"Erm, yes, why?"

"Your expletive outburst."

"Oh, right." It seemed so petty. "I'm having a pretty crappy morning, and someone's had the last tea bag without requisitioning more. I really need a cuppa. No, scratch that, I *need* a pint of wine."

"Oh dear, at least it's Friday, weekends are never a bad thing." He smiled.

"This one might be." I sulkily closed the cupboard and left my empty cup in the sink. "I'm being forced into another blind date, this time by my mother. If this were medieval times, I'd have been married off at thirteen to the first man who took an interest." I don't think I could have sounded any gloomier if I'd tried. He must think I'm a proper miserable sod.

"Are you not even a little bit excited?" He walked across the kitchen and stood next to me. "You never know, he might be an all right guy."

"Would you trust your mother to find you someone you'd like?"

"Hmm, fair point. Look, it might not be as bad as the picture you're painting in your head. And if it is… get a friend to call you with a problem or emergency so you *have* to leave as quickly as you can." He did some air quotes as he said "problem".

"Yeah." I smiled. "I never thought of that." I had seen that done a few times in movies and on TV, I don't know why Sarah and I never used that trick. It would have saved me from a lot of painfully dull, disastrous dates.

"I'm glad I could help." Zack's smile could make me feel better in any situation. "Anyway, I've been called back to the main office, so I need to go." He put his jacket on and picked up his bag. "I'm not sure when I'll be back out. Good luck for tomorrow. I hope it goes well."

"Thank you. Have a good weekend."

"You too."

He opened the door and with one final beautiful smile, he was gone. That was a miniature treat to boost the rest of my day. I was still pissed that I couldn't have a cuppa, but it would be lunchtime soon so I could go out and buy something then. If I could create a photo memory of Zack's smile then that should help me get through the rest of my day. I could even try to stretch it out to last me all of the next day too.

I hung out in the kitchen for longer than I should have done. If I was going to be deprived of some caffeine then they could all be deprived of me doing any proper work for the rest of the morning. Honestly, I only dared to stay in there until five minutes after I should have been back. No one seemed to notice me as I returned to my desk. Although when I got there, there was something odd by my keyboard. In front of it was a Costa takeaway cup, a small bag and a piece of paper. I picked up the paper and read the message.

I hope this cheers you up, try to have a good afternoon – Zack

I think my heart just exploded.

In the cup was a steaming hot tea and inside the bag was a little gingerbread man. Suddenly my face became adorned with a little giddy schoolgirl's grin. It was the best present I'd ever got.

I sat down before anyone noticed my ridiculous smile that would *not* be disappearing anytime soon. I logged back on to my computer and drafted him an email.

Thank you for the tea, much appreciated! I owe you one

Delete. Too much excitement.

Hey, thanks so much for the tea and biscuit. You've no idea how…

Delete. Too much information.

Thank you :) X

That would do nicely. I took a sip of my tea and put the biscuit in my bag for later. I thought very seriously about framing it, but it looked too nice not to eat. I glanced up from my computer to the hoard of miserable customers in front of me, huge smile across my face.

"Right then, who's next please?"

CHAPTER 15

*F*ive years ago, when I first walked into this office, I had no idea what I was letting myself in for. The title "Customer Service Advisor" seemed very vague, and the board of people interviewing me didn't give me much detail of the people I would be dealing with or what I would be assisting them with.

"The clients come in for help with a variety of local related matters. It can sometimes feel challenging, but you'll find it to be very rewarding," they had said. It was advertised as a very positive place to work where I would be making a difference in people's lives for all local authority matters at a front-line level. I'd be working alongside a team in a public office where anyone could walk through the door. Absolutely anyone. And whilst I soon discovered they meant absolutely anyone, pleasant or otherwise, my first day was when I spotted some very interesting eye candy.

"And then you click this button." Cheryl had been assigned as my trainer for the first day to show me a few things. "It just submits it to the back office who then pass on the fly tipping report to the Waste Management department. And hey ho, it gets cleared within the week. Easy enough, right? Are you all right, love?"

My eyes had drifted to the guy who walked in through the main doors. He'd smiled at me and then disappeared down the corridor.

"Who was that guy?" I asked. He was smartly dressed so didn't look like any of the customers I'd seen that day. "Does he work here too?" I wouldn't mind if he wanted to show me a thing or two. Work related matters, of course.

"Oh that's Zack. Very nice to look at. I'm old enough to be his mother so off limits to the likes of me. He comes out every now and then. Works for Asset Management. So if a customer ever comes in asking about buying or renting council property or land, he's a handy person to know. So, sometimes we get people in wanting to complain about dog fouling. In that case…"

Asset management. I'll look into that and see if it's a suitable job for me. There may be redeployment opportunities in the near future.

As soon as lunchtime came around that day, I was starving. I had good intentions in those early days and brought a lunch in with me. Ham and salad sandwich, an Activia yoghurt and a little Tupperware with some grapes. Yes, I was relatively healthy at one point, believe it or not.

"You can take up to an hour for your lunch," Angela told me. "You can hang out in the kitchen or go for a walk. We're in the town centre which can be dangerous on payday, but handy at Christmas. Have some lunch and I'll see you when you've finished." Angela led the way into the kitchen and Zack was already in there, eating a salad. "Ah, Zack, I didn't know you were out here today. Although I've been shut away in the office all morning. How you doing? This is Jennifer, our new starter."

"Hey," he smiled. "Welcome to the mad house."

"Thank you." I hoped I wasn't blushing, but wow his smile was magic.

"Right, I need to get back on that phone." She headed back to the doorway. "I'll see you in a bit, Jennifer."

The door closed behind her and I didn't know what to do with myself. Zack was tucking into a chicken salad. Also in a Tupperware. He brought his own homemade lunch with him too, we could have been a match made in heaven. Unless it was made by his mother or, even worse, a girlfriend.

I collected my food from the fridge and awkwardly sat down at the table opposite him. I had no idea what to say. Should I talk to him? What would I talk to him about? He was very nice looking though. I wanted to look busy, or like I had some kind of life, so I pulled my phone from my pocket and opened Facebook, but I soon wish I hadn't.

"Ah, bugger," I didn't mean to say that out loud.

"Everything okay?"

"No, well, fictionally no. Someone's put a spoiler on Facebook from last night's *Game of Thrones* episode, but I haven't seen it yet."

"Oh, don't," he shook his hands. "Please, I'm two episodes behind. I'm avoiding all media outlets until I can catch up. You're a fan, though?"

"Oh my God, yes, I'll be gutted when it finishes."

"Ha, I've finally got someone to chat about it with. No one here watches it anyway. What else do you watch?"

And so, for the next few years, we shared our views, likes and dislikes of all the leading shows on Sky, Netflix and Prime. That seemed to be the extent of our relationship. Well, until the gingerbread man anyway. Progress was progress.

When he finished his lunch, he rinsed the tub in the sink and left it on the draining board. I'd barely started my sandwich as I didn't want to risk talking to him with bits of lettuce in my mouth. Talking to him with food lodged in my mouth, that *would* be embarrassing.

"Right, I only get half an hour so I'll get back out there. Chat to you soon, yeah?" he smiled at me again. This was going to be dangerous.

71

"Yeah, chat to you soon."

And with that, he left me alone in the kitchen, with only my inappropriate thoughts of him bending me over a desk for company.

Sarah text me later that evening.

How was your first day? Xx

Oh Sarah... I need to tell you about Zack...X

And the rest was history.

CHAPTER 16

"*He* fancies you!" Sarah's voice boomed at me down the phone when I called her that evening and told her all about my little gift from Zack. "That's the sweetest thing. He proper fancies you!"

"It's possible for someone to be nice without it meaning anything." I was in the middle of hunting through my kitchen for something to eat. The gingerbread man was still in my bag. I decided to save it until my last cuppa before bed. "What if it's a 'pay it forward' thing? I now need to go out and do a good deed to someone else."

"Helping a blind man cross a road is a good deed, dropping a heap of clothes at a charity shop is a good deed, buying you a tea AND a biscuit, as well as taking the time to write you a note, is a hint. A hint that he likes you. You need to ask him out."

"I don't ask people out. That's a guy thing. Anyway, if he liked me..."

"Yes, blah blah blah he'd ask you out, the whole *'He's Just Not That Into You'* thing."

"It's true though." I slammed the fridge door shut. I was

getting zero inspiration for tonight's tea and getting very frustrated by my hungry belly.

"What are you doing?" Sarah asked. "All I can hear is banging."

"Looking for something to eat. No matter how many times I look in the fridge, it's still only milk, a bag of grated cheddar, which is possibly out of date, and a carrot." I'm not sure how the carrot got there to be honest.

"It's Friday night, why aren't you getting your Chinese?"

"Erm, I'm going off it I think." I hadn't dared to tell her about my rendezvous with Dan the previous weekend and my flatulence issues brought on by eating left over Chinese food. No one needs to know about that. "Anyway, what can our codeword be for when I need an escape tomorrow?"

"Gingerbread man."

"Maybe something a little easier to text to you unnoticed from under the table."

"Tea. That's easy enough."

"Right, 'tea', so when I text you, you *have* to call me straight away! Promise me!"

"I promise. What time are you meeting him? What's his name again?"

"Rob. And I'm meeting him at eleven at Costa. How imaginative for an artist. I'd have expected a vegan café or something."

"It beats the time when that Nigel you met wanted to take you to McDonald's for a first date."

"Ha! Tell me about it." Nigel started chatting me up at a bar a few years ago when Sarah and I went out one evening. He seemed great, very funny if not a little immature. And then when his offer of a Big Mac was presented to me, Sarah overheard and dragged me away.

I could eat a Big Mac now. I opened the fridge again hoping the food fairy had delivered a freshly made lasagne or chicken pie or anything I could throw in the oven to eat but, alas... It's official, I'm Mother Hubbard. "I don't know what I'm going to eat. I'm starving."

"Have you got any bread? Just make some toast. Or, now this is a crazy idea, nip to the shop and buy something you can cook! You can't go wrong with some soup."

"Soup? I can't make soup, who do you think I am?" Is she crazy? I live off takeaways and leftover takeaways. I don't know the first thing about making soup.

"I think even your culinary skills stretch to buying a tin of soup and heating it in the microwave. I honestly don't know how you've survived living on your own all these years."

"I'm a walking enigma." I checked the cupboards again.

"Right, hun, I need to go. I've got to get ready for this party at Max's office. I might be texting the codeword to you at some point. Ring me tomorrow night and tell me all about this Rob fella."

"I'll probably be texting you at quarter past eleven. Have a good night."

"You too, bye."

I hate being hungry. It makes me very grumpy. Which means if I don't get any food down me by my date with Rob, he'll be texting his own friends to get him out of a disaster date. I attempted one final look in the freezer. There was some mince that I bought a year ago when I thought about attempting to make a cottage pie, that never happened. It's possibly the reason I have a carrot in my fridge.

There was a bag of frozen vegetables from when I talked myself into healthy eating two years ago. I never quite got round to that, hence the unopened bag. I pulled them both out of the freezer to throw away and that was when I saw it. It had been hiding under the frozen veg. A pepperoni pizza. I'm saved!

CHAPTER 17

As I approached Costa Coffee I realised I had no idea what Rob looked like. Why didn't my mother give me a full description of him? What if he doesn't even turn up? Or, even worse, what if he's the perfect guy and it's my mother who found him for me? I'll never be able to live that down. She'd never let it go either. She'd be so smug at the wedding.

Town was always busy on a Saturday. I walked past mothers with unruly children, teenagers trying to look cool with their vapes, and a homeless guy hovering by the entrance. I survived my walk past the obstacles and looked around at all the tables. There were a few empty ones I could sit at, but I thought I'd best check for a single guy that could resemble a man waiting for a blind date first.

I didn't know how I would spot him, what does an artist look like? Would he be covered in paint? Would he be carrying a paint palette? Whatever he might look like, he definitely was not there yet. There weren't any singletons at any of the tables. I glanced at the door and noticed the homeless man was staring at me through the glass. What was his problem? I spied an empty table hidden in the corner out of view of the homeless man so quickly made my way there out of his sight. What a weirdo.

I decided it would be rude to order a drink before Rob got there so I pulled out my phone and started browsing Instagram. There was nothing exciting to look at but at least it was passing the time. A lot of my friends from school and university were on there, showcasing their families or exciting careers. My feed was filled with photos of Bing, there was the odd photo of me but not many.

It was safe to say my miniscule number of followers didn't get much amazement from what I posted. However, seeing their working trips to Dubai or family holidays to New Zealand made me feel, what are the words I'm looking for? Oh yes, no one likes a show-off.

I don't know what made me look up, but there he was, the homeless guy again. However, this time he was inside and looking around. What was he looking for? A few people noticed and looked as confused as I did. He caught my eye. He was looking for me. He sheepishly lifted his hand to wave at me. I kept my head down but it didn't work, he started to walk towards me. Why do I never attract the Henry Cavills of the world?

"Jenny?"

How does he know my name?

"Yes, can I help you?" I put my phone in my pocket in case he decided to snatch it.

"I'm Rob." He reached out his hand to shake mine.

Oh. My. God.

"Oh, hello." I shook one of his hands before I spotted the state of them. They were moist with sweat and stained with muck and his fingernails were a vile shade of yellow. The rest of him was not any better. His black, greasy hair was shoulder length and very dishevelled. Half of it was resting on his shoulder and the other half was up in a man bun. I don't believe in men having a man bun, it just didn't look right.

His jumper was something else completely. It resembled something that a grandmother would knit for you for Christmas that you would only wear on the day to be kind and then put it in the back of the wardrobe as soon as you could. It was multicoloured and multi-damaged. I lost count of the number of holes it had. Why would someone wear such a thing on a first date? And what was that smell? It was like a combination of broccoli and eggs.

My mother had done this on purpose. She'd decided that I'd left it too late for a decent man so had to end up with the dregs, like at the bottom of a tube of Pringles when all that's left are the broken ones. I don't deserve a full Pringle.

"Do you want a coffee then?" he asked, with very little enthusiasm. I had to hold my breath as the broccoli and eggs aroma hit my defenceless nostrils. I leaned backwards to get as far away from it as possible.

"Erm, please. Mocha. Small. Thanks." I had to rub my hand over my nose to help me to open my mouth and speak to him. I didn't want to breathe in any of the air that surrounded him.

I pulled out my phone, time for my saviour Sarah to call me with an emergency. I typed "tea" into a message to Sarah ready to hit send as soon as Rob sat down opposite me. I wished I'd found a bigger table for us. This small one meant we were sat too close together. People sitting nearby were suddenly aware of the smell and were looking in my direction.

As soon as I saw him pick up the tray of drinks and head back towards me, I hit "send" and left my phone on the table so he could see that I was getting a genuine phone call and that I was not faking it. All I had to do was wait. It shouldn't be too long, and then I could make my quick getaway.

"It's not cheap here, is it? There you go." He lifted my cup by the handle and placed it in front of me before taking his seat opposite. I'd have to avoid that handle.

"Thank you." That jumper was really disgusting. If anyone was to look at us, they would think that I was his support worker. And to think, I was panicking this morning thinking I would be late as I had to quickly rush to change my tights because the first pair had a ladder in them. I should have avoided tights altogether and left my stubbly legs on display. We'd look a bit more suited then.

"This is different," he began. "I don't often go on dates." Shocking. He lifted his drink and loudly slurped his coffee. "Ahhh, that's hot." He looked up at the window behind me and squinted. "Do you mind if we move somewhere else? The light's really blinding."

"Oh," I looked behind me at the tiny window, "erm..."

"It's just that my house is really dark because of Draco and Severus. They don't like it too light, you see. So being out like this hurts my corneas." As he squinted his eyes and screwed his face up, I noticed his last few remaining teeth were almost brown.

"Why don't we swap sides?" I could see there were some seats at the back of the coffee shop, but the last thing I wanted was to walk down there and be seen with him. At least here we were kind of hidden.

We both stood up to swap sides before I realised that this clever idea of mine meant I would be sitting where he had already sat. As I held my breath to pass him, I looked at the plastic chair which already had a tiny sweat mark on it. He sat down while I delayed sitting for as long as possible, hoping the sweat would dry quickly. Why hadn't Sarah called me yet?

"Thanks. That's much better." He picked up his cup and took another loud slurp. "This stuff is always expensive, don't you think? It would've been cheaper to make you a coffee at my house."

As tempting as that sounds… "It's nice though, isn't it? There's always a nice atmosphere in here and you can't beat the coffee."

"Yes, you can, it's seventy-nine pence for Tesco's value coffee, a full jar. Do you know what this cost me? I could've bought ten jars for what I've spent in here."

"Do you want me to pay for my own? I can give you the money for mine." I reached down to pick up my bag. The strap was touching his leg. I saw his brown chord trousers were also full of holes. There was an odd stain going up his leg. I would have to burn this bag as soon as I got home.

"No, no. It's fine. I'll have to pick up another shift at Burger King to stop myself going into debt."

"So," must change the subject, "my mum tells me you're an artist. What's that like?"

"Yeah, I paint things. Mostly Draco and Severus."

"You're a Slytherin then, are you? I've always liked Gryffindor, bit of a cliché but you can't help loving the heroes." He stared at me, blankly. Did I just speak in Chinese?

"What do you mean?" How does he not understand me?

"Draco and Severus, they're in Slytherin, aren't they? You must love them if you paint only those two characters. Do you ever paint anyone else from the films?"

"Eh?"

Seriously, am I speaking another bloody language?

"You've seen *Harry Potter*, haven't you? You must have done if you're painting two of the leading characters?"

"Harry Potter?!" He let out an almighty snort of a laugh. It made me jump. A few people around us stared. "Harry bloody Potter. I've been called many things but a Harry Potter fan? Don't insult me."

"So why the hell are you painting two of the most important characters from the whole bloody series?" Come on, Sarah, hurry up! I glanced down at my phone, but the black screen was staring back at me.

"Draco and Severus are my snakes!" Duh, how could I not know this... "Draco means 'serpent' in Ancient Greek and Severus means 'stern' in Latin." My Ancient Greek wasn't perfect but, damn, I clearly needed to brush up on my Latin too. "It's nothing to do with those films."

"The books are actually really good, you should give them a try." I had to defend my favourite wizarding world. I grew up with it. I remember waiting excitedly every year for each new book to be released. I'm not ashamed to admit that I'm still waiting for my Hogwarts acceptance letter. Who isn't?

"I don't read." He stared at me intensely as he said those words, not even blinking. "It's all a conspiracy."

"Excuse me?"

"Yeah, it's all a plot." He leaned back in his chair and his expression turned deadly serious. "The government want to brainwash us, you see, make us read these books to sway us into thinking a certain way, living a particular life, to fall in line."

"Oh," suddenly I was wishing that we were sat in the middle of the coffee shop after all, in full view so I had plenty of witnesses to protect me, "I didn't realise that authors were being paid by the government in order to coerce us to 'fall in line.'" I wonder what part of an eleven-year-old boy going to wizarding school has to do with the government. I hope J K Rowling got paid enough to create such a deceptive government weapon.

"They all work for the government." He lowered his voice to a whisper. "There are spies everywhere. Even in here, there are hidden cameras and microphones everywhere, spying on us, listening to every word we say."

I don't know why I looked around for these hidden cameras, this guy was insane. If Sarah didn't call me soon I'd be fearing for my life.

"So, erm." I was at a loss for words. I needed to change the subject before MI5 stormed Costa to arrest him. "Do you have any other pets?"

"No, they were taken away by the RSPCA. Another government-led operation. I had more snakes, but they were *really* intelligent. The government found out and took them off me. They were scared, you see, that I'd train them up and bring down parliament."

"Erm… okay." I was waiting for the punchline, a laugh, anything remotely human from this modern day Guy Fawkes.

"I'll find the cameras. They're in my house somewhere. I don't know where, or how many there are, but I'll get them."

I lifted my cup, avoiding the handle he'd touched, and took a long sip of my drink. This had to be a dream. Either that or I was being pranked somehow. Sarah was going to jump out of a cupboard and shout "Gotcha!" any moment. I took a deep breath before placing my cup back down to resume this date.

"So, you work at Burger King? What's that like?"

"Monotonous. But it pays the bills."

"I've never been a fan of Burger King. McDonald's, though, I do love their cheeseburgers."

"Pah!" he said, loudly. A woman was about to pass us with her young son. She put her hands on his shoulders and led him a different way, so they wouldn't have to walk directly past our table. "McDonald's." Rob was shaking his head.

"Let me guess, another government organisation?"

"Exactly. They put chemicals in the food. It's mixed in with the oils, so the burgers and chips absorb them properly. Then you eat them, and it makes its way into your system permanently. The food is all rotten, but you wouldn't know, because of the chemicals making you think you're enjoying what you eat."

"Okay then." I was flabbergasted. I can't say I didn't make an effort with conversation on this date.

"I'll be back in a minute."

He stood and walked down to the toilets. I watched as people moved to one side as he walked past them to make sure they wouldn't come into contact with him. Then their expressions changed as they were hit by his smell. I used this opportunity to pick up my phone and call Sarah.

"Hello?" she answered.

"Sarah? What the hell?" I angrily whispered. "Where's my emergency phone call?"

"Shit, I'm sorry! I thought I heard my phone bleep in my bag but I've been busy. Was it really bad then? Are you on your way home?"

"No, I'm still here. He's gone to the gents. It's awful. Seriously. I'd go on a second date with Gerard if it meant I could get out of this one. Will you bloody phone me so I can leave?"

"Yes! Yes, I will. When do you want me to call you?"

"Give it two minutes, then make sure you call me."

"I will, I will, I'm so sorry!"

"Yeah, yeah. Bye."

I quickly put my phone back down on the table in time to see him walking over. I couldn't help but wonder if he was the type of guy who washed his hands. For some reason, I doubted it very much.

As soon as he sat down, I could smell the eggs and broccoli again. It seemed stronger than it was before, like it was seeping out of his skin. He must have seen the look on my face.

"What's the matter?"

"I had an odd whiff of something. I can't put my finger on what it is." I didn't know how else to tell him that he stank.

"It's probably these you can smell." He reached into his pocket and pulled out a small bundle, I couldn't tell what it was. "I've got them for Draco and Severus."

I looked closer, wondering why he was carrying balls of string in his pocket and why they would appeal to snakes. And then I saw that one of the balls had eyes and whiskers.

"You're carrying mice in your pocket?!" I jumped back in my seat. "Why are you carrying mice?"

He laughed. "Don't worry, they're dead so can't harm you. I found them on my way here."

With his other hand he picked one of them up by the tail and hung it in front of him. He looked like he was going to eat it. I realised that he'd have had them in his pocket before he got here. He would have handled them before I shook his hand. I suddenly felt very sick.

"I have to go." I reached down and grabbed my bag from under the table.

"What's the matter?" He looked genuinely confused, but I didn't want to hang around for him another second, nor wait for Sarah's phone call.

"Goodbye."

I quickly headed out the door and ran down the cobbled street to Superdrug so I could buy some hand sanitizer. I felt disgusting. I felt filthy. I wouldn't let my hand touch anything. Not until I had either cleaned it or chopped it off. As I nudged the door open with my shoulder, my phone rang. I answered it with a knuckle then held it to my ear with the other shoulder.

"Jenny! You have to come home quick!"

"You can save it, Sarah, I already left."

"Really? Already? What happened?"

I had picked some sanitizer and paid for it with my one clean hand on the self-checkout with my phone still tucked between my head and shoulder, I had filled Sarah in on the whole experience. As I told her about the mice, she started to gag down the phone.

"Oh, Jenny," I could tell she was trying not to retch, "I can't believe you lasted as long as you did. What was your mother thinking setting you up with him?"

"Probably a delayed punishment for something from my childhood. I don't know. But I need to go home and stand under the shower for the rest of the day and possibly bleach my hands." I squirted loads of gel into my palm and then rubbed it all over my hands and even up my wrists. "What are you doing tomorrow? I feel like I haven't seen you for ages."

"I know, I've been so busy lately. But we're with Max's parents tomorrow and I can't get away. Are you free next Friday night?"

"No, I have this awards thing for work. I need to be there, my meal's been paid for."

"Okay, I'll call you one night this week and we can catch up. Be careful with the bleach, don't melt your hands off."

"After touching Rob, that might not be a bad thing!"

CHAPTER 18

My skin was red from my extra long and extra hot shower that evening. I had to scrub every essence of my date with Rob from myself. Clothes went straight into a hot wash and I wiped my handbag down with antibacterial wipes I use to clean the kitchen worktop after Bing decides to do his butt-licking yoga up there. He took quite an interest in me when I got home. Could probably smell that I'd had dead rodents near me.

When I checked my phone I had four missed calls from my mother. She hadn't grasped how to send a text message yet which suited me fine. I wouldn't be in a rush to call her back anyway.

Fresh air was needed now to clear out my lungs from potential fungal infection, so I decided to make use of the garden. I slipped on some comfy lounge wear, grabbed my cup of tea with a bag of Maltesers and slid open the patio door. Bing took this to mean we were racing to be the first one outside and sought to sabotage any victory of mine and ran between my legs. It was almost a tea and Malteser catastrophe but luckily I am well practised in the art of cat antics so nothing was spilled.

I placed the cup and bag on the little table I got from The

Range in the sale last year and folded out two chairs. One for me to sit on and one for my feet. The air was quite warm and at this time of the evening, the sun reached this top corner of my garden. Bing disappeared behind some old plant pots, probably got the taste for mice now so is on the hunt.

I'd no sooner plonked my phone on the table too when it started buzzing again. It wasn't my mother this time, it was her leading henchman.

"Will," I said as I answered. "How's it going?"

"Hey, sis, what's new? Been on any interesting dates lately?"

"She told you?"

"Why do you think I'm calling?" he chuckled. "You're ignoring her calls. She thinks she's sent you off to the man of your dreams and you've eloped. So... how'd it go?"

His tone seemed suspicious. "Did you know about him? If you knew she was sending me off on a date with him and you never warned me, I'll kill you."

"Ha! I had no idea until ten minutes ago when mum called me with a mission of finding you. She'd have had me at Gretna Green if you'd ignored me too. So how is Rob? I haven't seen him for years. I was at college with him, you know."

"You were friends with him?" Gross.

"No, no. I didn't say I was friends with him, I said I was at college with him. At the same time as him anyway. And I witnessed his expulsion for stealing one of the stuffed owls in the old hall."

"So he's been perfect marriage material for some time then? Mum should have set me up with him sooner. I could be happily married with all those kids like you. Speaking of which, Mum proudly told me you're having a girl. Big congrats and all that."

"Thank you, Liz is over the moon. We both are and the boys are excited to have a baby sister."

I sipped some tea from my cup and heard the scratching of

sharp claws skating along the patio and into the house. "Bloody hell."

"What's up?" Will asked.

"Bing. He's just chased something into the house and I've no idea what it is. I'm sure I'll discover it in a shoe or the bath at some point." I heard him let out a howl from somewhere inside. "And now he's doing his wild jungle call. Psycho mode has commenced."

"I love Bing, he's ace. You picked a good one for entertainment. Speaking of the house, how is my home doing?"

"Erm, whose home?" I popped a Malteser into my mouth and let it crunch down the phone.

"Come on, that'll always be my house too. We grew up there with Dad."

"Yes, and I bought your share which meant you could pay for that extension in your mansion." When dad died, I couldn't bear to see the house be sold on to someone else. So with my inheritance and small amount of savings, I had enough to take out a mortgage and buy out my brother.

He chose to ignore me. "I need to go in the loft actually, I'm sure I've got some old PlayStation games up there. Proper retro now. They'll be worth a fortune."

"Yeah you could sell them and convert your second garage into a spa or something."

He lowered his voice. "Don't give Liz any ideas, she's already got eyes on my office for a playroom for the kids. So, anyway, back to our house."

"Actually, now you mention it, it does feel like 'our' old house. Every time Bing leaves me a parcel in his litter box, and the aroma fills the landing, I do have flashbacks to staying here on the weekends with you."

"Ha ha, you're hilarious."

I laughed as I popped another Malteser into my mouth.

"Anyway," he said. "I can report to Mum that you're alive, you haven't eloped, and that all is good, you're just on strike from speaking to her, yes?"

"Yes, that should get the message across."

"Okay. Right, I'd best go. Liz is going through her pregnancy sickness phase so I said I'd get the boys to bed. Come visit soon, okay?"

"I'll try," I promised. "Bye."

I should investigate whatever Bing brought into the house but there was still some sun shining on my face which felt really nice. I should spend more time out here, it's not a bad sized garden. Every year I promise to get a landscape gardener in to make the most of the space but it never happens. The most effort I've made is buying this table and chair set which will do for now.

It had been a while since I looked at what was going on in the world of Facebook, so I swiped open the app. I had a few notifications.

Sarah tagged you in a post.

Sarah commented on your post.

Lewis sent you a friend request.

Lewis wants to send you a message.

Lewis? Who the heck was Lewis?

CHAPTER 19

*L*ewis is *not* my cousin. He isn't. Not technically. No, he just isn't. So what if he's my dad's half-sister's nephew? He is *not* my cousin. So what if he came to every family event and was sat with my brother and me at the cousins table? It doesn't mean anything. He was always quite geeky back when we were younger. He had an overbite, acne and those glasses you'd get for free from Specsavers. A bit Harry Potter-esque if you can picture it. You may have heard of Harry Potter if you're about my age or from planet Earth.

Lewis was never someone you could imagine having the confidence to introduce himself to a girl or be in a relationship. He was always into gaming. I remember when he got the PlayStation 1 and brought it around to our house. He and William would play Cool Boarders or Twisted Metal World Tour for hours and hours.

Then came along the PlayStation 2 and their games advanced to Grand Theft Auto and Gran Turismo as they got older. Lewis was a bit obsessed with the mechanics behind the game itself and how it was made. I remember we didn't see him for a while because his parents had grounded him for dismantling his

PlayStation 2 to see if he could rebuild it to full working order. It turns out he could, as it happens, but his parents were furious when they walked in to see it in a hundred pieces. I can't even rewire a plug, never mind rebuild a computer console.

We haven't actually spoken to each other in years as families, as in family friends, not relations, drift apart as time goes by. So I didn't even click when Lewis requested to send me a message on Facebook. I had no idea who it was at first. Just another random guy wanting to send me vulgar messages.

However, when I saw the profile picture, I was distracted by this Tom Ellis lookalike, circa the Lucifer era. This hot, seemingly nice, guy wanted to send me a message. He had to be a catfish because no one this hot would reach out to me, not with my profile picture showing me clutching onto two cocktails, my lips practically stretching out trying to put both straws in my mouth. It wasn't my proudest moment, and not my best photo, but it drives my mum mad so you've got to pick your battles.

After a few flirtatious, friendly messages back and forth, I finally clicked who he was. It was Lewis! And asking me out for coffee too... very eager to meet up with me.

"He's your cousin!" Sarah bellowed in horror down the phone when she called me mid-week. "That's just wrong. I don't care what he looks like, you *cannot* go on a date with him."

"He's *not* my cousin. I happened to grow up with him–"

"Yes, as your cousin!"

"As a close family friend," I said calmly. "But I haven't seen him since I was sixteen. He was eighteen and going off to university. We drifted apart. What's wrong with a coffee date and catch-up?"

"Nothing, unless you're imagining climbing on top of him later."

Did I mention that after we added each other on Facebook I happened to have a gander through his photos and there were one or two which were quite... I don't really know what noise came out of my mouth as I was scrolling through them but it clearly offended Bing who gave me a dirty look and left the room. Rude.

"He's not my cousin!" I'd felt the need to shout after Bing as he ran away from my presence. I'm so defensive about that very obvious fact though. I'm sure if I was to do my DNA check, I would share more genetics with my dentist than I do Lewis. Maybe.

"So when's the big family reunion?" Sarah asked.

"Tomorrow after work." I chose to ignore her mistake, there is no "family" anything. The more I fought it, the more it looked like I also felt ashamed, which I didn't. I absolutely didn't. Because, as I may have mentioned once or twice, we are not related. "I've got an early finish so I can get changed in the toilets and then head into Halifax, we're meeting at Café Mille. Pricey, but he's offered to pay."

"That *is* a pricey place." Finally she seemed impressed. "I hope you're wearing your best coat."

"I may have dug out the Marks and Spencer one especially for the occasion."

The only place this black suede coat was safe from Bing's white fur and hungry claws was in a bag, in a suitcase, in the loft, right at the back.

"You definitely mean business. Are you going to tell your mum?"

"Absolutely not, are you mad?"

Sarah laughed. "Is that because you're somehow pre-empting that she will have the same opinion as me?"

"The moment you and my mother share the same opinion is the moment I divorce you and move to Alaska to live an isolated life."

"You wouldn't last, you hate the snow."

That was true.

CHAPTER 20

I parked at the bottom of town and made my way up to meet Lewis. It didn't take me long to spot him. He stood out with his height and perfectly slicked back hair. He had spotted me too and smiled a perfect, very straight pearly white smile in my direction. I did wonder if he had done some photoshopping on his pictures to clear up his complexion, but even in real life he looked like someone out of a Max Factor advert. I'm not even sure whether I walked or floated towards him but somehow, out of nowhere, he was just inches away from me.

"Jenny." He held out his arms and pulled me into him for a very long, satisfying hug. The smell, oh my. Even my ovaries could smell him. I could almost feel them lining up the eggs to launch at him. No worries of deformities or webbed feet if we ever did procreate because that only happened between blood relations. "It's so good to see you."

"I know." I pulled back away from his grasp, reluctantly. "It's been far too long."

"Shall we go in?"

I didn't even realise we were outside Café Mille. Clearly I'd floated there too.

He opened the door, allowing me to enter first, but then led the way knowingly to the booths at the back where there was one free just for us. I removed my jacket, gently folding it to sit beside me. It was known as the best coat for a reason. I've never spent so much money on an item of clothing. Even with the fifty-pound voucher I used, it still cost me over a hundred pounds of my own money. It is a good coat for those special occasions though when I want to make an impression.

As he took his seat opposite me, I realised how nervous I felt. When we were younger, and he wasn't involved in some computer game with my brother, we got on so well. Really well. We'd laugh together so much, almost cackling to the point we couldn't breathe. Our parents once kicked us out of our uncle's funeral because we got the giggles sitting next to each other.

Not "our" uncle. That's wrong, and would imply... you know. It was *his* uncle. My sort-of uncle. Something to do with my dad... we are *not* cousins.

"Jenny?"

"Yes? Sorry?"

Had he been talking this entire time I was almost drooling over him?

"What would you like to drink?" he asked, nodding his perfect head towards the waiter standing next to me. Lewis's hair fell into his eyes as he did this and he flicked it back out of the way. Now I was in a Herbal Essences advert.

"I'll have a latte, thank you." I wasn't even a big fan of lattes, but it sounded a little more exotic than a plain white coffee. This place was very over the top with its prices. I could have ordered three large cappuccinos in Costa for what Lewis was about to pay for my one latte. I wonder how many shifts at Burger King Rob would have to do to compensate a coffee date here.

"That's great, and for you, sir?"

"Could I get a triple espresso coffee, with milk but make it half full fat and half semi skimmed, extra hot, hazelnut syrup and one sweetener, thank you."

"Very good, sir." The waiter walked away, totally not bothered about the most bizarre coffee order I'd ever heard. The waiter didn't even write it down.

I'd already forgotten what he ordered. A triple espresso with what? "That's quite an order," I said.

Lewis smiled. "I was in Tuscany one year, or was it Milan? Somewhere over that way. Someone took me to a coffee tasting and now my palette is so refined I can't have just a plain coffee anymore."

A refined palette for coffee? I can tell the difference between Nescafe and Asda's own, does that count? First James the wine connoisseur and now Lewis, the coffeeisseur.

"Sounds like you've had some exotic holidays." I'd never consider Milan for a holiday, unless Jet2 decided to offer it as a package all-inclusive deal for probably the same value as the posh coat sitting next to me.

"Not holidays. Those trips were for work. They fly me all over the place."

I remember hearing he was studying computer gaming at university but I didn't think that would be the kind of career which meant travelling abroad to such places. Unless game launches had the same red-carpet treatment that movies had with celebrity appearances and the Press there taking photos. I don't remember seeing anything about work trips on his Facebook feed, however I was focusing on photos of his face at the time.

"Who do you work for?" It must be Nintendo, or someone as big.

"I'm the personal assistant to Rodrigo Ricci."

"Rodrigo Ricci?" If I had been sipping my overpriced latte there and then, I'm sure I would have spat it all over Lewis. "*The*

Rodrigo Ricci? Founder of *The Look* magazine? Fashion designer to the stars? The royals?"

"You've heard of him then." Lewis chuckled. He looked at me and I noticed his lips had parted slightly. There was a gap I was tempted to stick my finger in…

"Have I heard of him? I can't get enough of him. The dresses he had at the Oscars last year. How on earth did you get a job working for him? What happened to doing computery things?" I motioned typing on a computer keyboard because clearly that was necessary.

He smiled. "University changed my life. In quite a few ways, actually." He leaned back and his knee knocked mine as he crossed it over his other leg. Intentional? Must have been. Guys don't usually sit with their knees crossed over like that. "I started seeing someone, Jo, and my life altered almost overnight." Lewis's eyes twinkled. "Jo opened up my world in so many ways."

"Oh yeah?" I was trying to pay attention, or at least seem as though I was, but I was almost hypnotised by him. He had a slight bit of stubble on his face but it was perfectly shaped around his jaw line.

"Jo then took me on holiday and the people who I was suddenly surrounded by, and the clothes." He gestured his hands in front of himself. "That was when I realised how much I love fashion. And I'm good at it too. I helped co-ordinate Ricci's last catwalk, selecting designs and who would model them." I was still watching Lewis's hands and I noticed his nails were perfectly manicured. I was almost jealous of them, but also slightly mortified as my Rimmel nail varnish was all chipped and didn't look good next to his. He's still talking, I should listen. "And I've been so happy since. I changed my degree, got a master's too, spent a year in New York with Jo and I've never looked back."

"Wait." I leaned forward. "I think I've missed something. Is Jo still around then?"

"Jo, yes, it's short for Josef, and he's my fiancé."

Jenny, you absolute tit.

"Ah, I see." I try to disguise the blushes of embarrassment hoping he wouldn't notice. "Sorry, I didn't get that at first. You're engaged, wow!"

"Yes, we made it official last year. I'm surprised your mum didn't tell you?"

"She's usually eager to tell me when someone is getting married so I'm surp–"

"He's here!" Lewis slid out from our booth to greet an equally neat and beautiful man who was clearly and visibly (to anyone but me, apparently) a fellow homosexual man. If I couldn't tell by his lilac alligator print silk shirt then their prolonged kiss would have given the game away ever so slightly.

"Jenny, I want you to meet Jo." Lewis's happiness was clear. He was in love. How could I not be happy for him?

"Jenny." Jo slid in next to me before I had a chance to stand up. "I've heard so much about you. I can't believe I'm finally meeting the favourite cousin."

Cousin. Yes. Who would even think about dating a cousin? That's just wrong.

"Oh, we've had some good times." I had to redeem myself, if only in my eyes. I had to let this wash over me and be myself. Live up to Jo's expectations of a favourite cousin. Wait until I tell my mum that I'm the favourite over my perfect brother. She will be shocked. Our coffees finally arrived and Lewis ordered a non-fat decaf cappuccino for Jo.

"Has he asked you yet?" Jo grabbed my hand. "Please say yes, it would make us so happy."

"To what?" What do they want from me? To be flower girl at their celebrity-filled wedding? Would it be here in England or on some exotic Greek island? Oh my, what if there are models there? I'll have to lay off the takeaways. And chocolate. And full fat milk. Was it too late to exchange my latte for a glass of water?

"I haven't had chance to ask her yet," Lewis said. "We've barely even been sat here five minutes."

"Colour me curious," I said as Jo's grip on my hand intensified. It felt like I would have no chance of release unless I agreed to whatever they wanted. I was quite giddy actually. What could they possibly want from me?

"Okay…" Lewis began. "You can say no to this," although judging by the lack of blood supply in my fingers I wasn't too sure I could. "We were wondering… if there was any chance you might… like to be a surrogate for us."

My hand may as well have fallen off at that point and I wouldn't have noticed. Someone could actually have punched me in the ovaries and I wouldn't have noticed that either.

"You… what? You want me to what?"

"We thought long and hard. Every woman we know is already married with their own families." Another punch to the ovaries. "It might be too difficult for them to take it on. But with you being single." Double punch. "No real responsibilities." Triple punch. "And now in your thirties." *Strap me to a railway track at this point and leave me there.* "We thought you'd be the perfect candidate."

They genuinely think I would want to grow a tiny human for them. What is this, *The Handmaid's Tale*? And what do they mean by saying I have no responsibilities? They have clearly never seen what happens when a cat gets hungry. I mean, the great Cat Food Shortage of 2019 was traumatic for both Bing and myself. I'd run out of biscuits for him so I promised to grab some on my way home from work if he was able to last a whole eight hours for me. He wasn't exactly wasting away. He, however, couldn't cope with that amount of time and decided to eat half of my slipper. So that night, I was down five pounds for a bag of cat food plus five hundred pounds in emergency vet bills. So, yes, actually, I do have responsibilities.

I fidgeted with my phone under the table with my free left

hand. The right was still trapped in Jo's grasp as they waited for my answer. I somehow managed to type a message to Sarah which either said "tea" or "twa". I have no idea which, but it worked. Moments later she called with the wonderful news that my house had flooded and I was needed there immediately.

Just three minutes later, after a very rushed, flushed and mushed goodbye, I was back walking down the high street to the safety of my car. My uterus was safe for now. Also, maintaining and paying for a car is also a responsibility. I'm a strong, independent woman who works and pays bills and a mortgage on my own. It's a small mortgage seeing as I inherited half the house from my late father so only had to buy the other half from my brother, but still, my payments have never been a minute late.

CALL ME! Sarah's text practically shouted.

"Don't ask," was my greeting to her. "Don't *even* ask. I'm minutes away from calling Gerard back for a second date as well as marriage and babies seeing as though being single in your thirties is a cry for help."

"What happened?"

I expected hysterical giggles. I expected comedy material for years to come. Sarah didn't laugh.

"How bloody dare they!" she said. "Expecting you to say yes like that, just because you're a single woman in your thirties?"

"I don't know what to say."

"You know who put them up to this, don't you?"

"Who?" And then the penny dropped. "I'll call you back."

I reached my car in time for an internal, verbal eruption. Swiping through my phone, I found my victim and called them.

"Hello?" she said, almost jovial.

"Mum, just the person I wanted to speak to. Apart from setting me up with reptile-loving weirdos because you have zero faith in my dating abilities, is there anything else you want to tell me?"

CHAPTER 21

*Z*ack lifted his hand to my face and stroked my chin, all the *while looking deep into my eyes. His face was so close to mine that I could see my reflection in his eyes. His other hand found my waist and pulled me in closer to him so that our bodies were touching. I could feel him against me, he wanted me. My tingles were out of control, I knew that as soon as he kissed me, I would explode on the spot. I had wanted this moment for years. I could smell him. I could almost taste him. He closed his eyes and moved his face slowly towards mine. I was ready...*

"Ouch!" Bing landed hard on my chest, waking me up from my dream. "Bing, you're such an ill-timed wanker!" I pushed him onto the floor and tried to get myself back to sleep, back to being with Zack, but it was no use. I was wide awake. Flustered, horny and lonely in my big bed.

I checked my phone to see what time it was. I had only fifteen minutes before my alarm would be going off. That would have been fifteen minutes of erotic dream lovemaking, where there was no fear or boundaries. I hate my cat. I'm also not very fond of my own mother. First setting me up with Rob who, I'm pretty sure, would one day kill me in my sleep and feed me to his snakes. And then she neglected to tell me she had been negotiating terms to rent my womb out to Lewis and his fiancé seeing as though I was showing no signs of planning to use it myself. I don't know why she is obsessed with the idea. My brother, dream child that he is, is about to produce his third offspring. Surely she doesn't need any more grandchildren?

Bing looked smug when I walked into my kitchen to make a cup of tea, unfazed by my mopey expression. He sat in front of his empty food dish expecting me to fill it.

"You can jog on." He yapped at me in response. "And before you even think about it, I've shut all the upstairs doors so you can't leave me any surprises for when I get back tonight."

He stood up and with a flick of the tail, which I'm sure is the cat equivalent of giving the finger, he turned and headed towards the door which I gladly opened to get rid of him. Once he was gone, I filled his food dish, hoping he could hear the biscuits hitting the bottom of the bowl from outside. *Yeah, how do you like that, cat?* I can be mean too.

I already hate the day. Not only did I miss out on a mind-blowing, subconscious orgasm, but it was my company's annual awards ceremony which I have to attend. Each year, different departments are invited along with the individuals who have been nominated. It is seen as a privilege, but our manager told us it was compulsory, so, regardless of whether we wanted to go or not, we didn't have a choice.

I didn't feel in the mood to go to work. If there was no ceremony I would have called in sick and had a day to myself. The conversation I had with my mum went as I expected, which meant I explained how her actions made me feel and she didn't listen to reason. It made its way back to my brother who'd been trying to call me all week. I'd been a bad sister and ignored his messages. *I will call him, I will. I'm just not in the mood yet.*

There was no point in coming home after work to rush to get changed and head back out again, so the whole team decided to hang back at the office to get ready there and share a taxi to the venue. I had carefully folded my black dress into a bag along with shoes and my make-up bag. I'd had a shower that morning, so my hair was looking fresh and glossy. If anything would make me smile, it was that my hair was actually behaving and doing what I wanted it to do.

"So, no one on our team's been nominated?" Cheryl asked Angela.

"That's right," Angela replied.

"But we still have to go?"

"That's right." Angela had had this conversation with us all at least once already this week and I could tell she was getting sick of repeating herself.

"But why?" Cheryl was in her fifties, but she whined like a petulant teenager. She was always the first to complain to Angela about anything and everything, no matter how petty.

"Look," Angela was in the ladies' toilets with us all getting ready now our working day was finally over. We were almost ready. "I know none of us want to go, but in the seven years I've worked here our team has never been invited. Funding's already low but if we snub tonight then they might cut our funding altogether. This is purely political." She threw her make-up back in her bag and pulled out a hairbrush. "Let's go, eat the free food, drink the wine, and then once the awards are handed out you can leave, that's all I ask."

Talk of free food and wine seemed to shut Cheryl up for now. It was only six though. We weren't due to be there until seven and a taxi would only take twenty minutes.

"What can we do before we set off? We've got ages yet. Do we nip to the pub for a quick one?" I asked while making sure my hair was still behaving after a long boring day.

"No," Angela said before Cheryl could suggest we nip to the Wetherspoons down the road. "If we head out now then I'll never get you all in that taxi. I brought a bottle of wine and a few beers with me. We can sit in the kitchen with the guys until the taxis come for us. Does that sound all right? Just don't tell the area manager we had alcohol on the premises, deal?"

Cheryl finally cracked a smile. "Sounds good to me!"

Once we were ready, we met the others in the kitchen and all had a drink before being led out to the taxis waiting for us. It was going to be a long night.

CHAPTER 22

"*And* that is why, with your continued hard work and dedication, I know that this time next year we can be stronger yet. Thank you for listening, now on to the awards." Our elderly Chief Executive finally took his seat away from the microphone.

That had to be the most boring speech I'd ever listened to. I lost count of how many times I'd yawned. Every time I did, Cheryl yawned back at me, which made me yawn again. It was a vicious circle yet managed to entertain us for the twenty minutes we had to endure empty words of hope for the company's future and lies of how much they appreciated all of our hard work.

Mr Leeming, the Managing Director, stepped forward to the microphone. "Thank you, Mr Moss. It is an absolute pleasure to have you here with us this evening." The lights from above were reflecting off his balding head, almost creating a disco ball effect due to the trickles of sweat making their way down his forehead.

"Arse kisser alert," Cheryl whispered to me. I wasn't expecting to hear that, I almost spat out my Prosecco, which left us both in a fit of giggles.

"Will you two stop giggling." Angela leaned over to us. "It's like sitting with children."

"Sorry, Angela," we both said as I wiped the Prosecco from my chin.

"Now, it is time for what we have all been waiting for," Mr Leeming continued, "our awards for esteemed achievements over the last twelve months. This year, I have the honour of presenting the awards and it gives me such pleasure to do so. Twenty-two years ago, I myself was at one of these events when I was a junior assistant working in Public Relations. I was there because I was presented with an award and look at me now." He smugly pointed at himself. "Hard work brings great results."

"And a shiny forehead," Cheryl whispered to me. I tried to conceal my laughter, but my bouncing shoulders gave me away and Angela scolded us again.

"Our first award is for outstanding attendance and punctuality…"

I didn't know how many awards there were to hand out, but I knew it was going to be a long-arse night. I looked around at the other tables wondering if anyone was actually enjoying themselves and they all looked as bored as we were. I didn't recognise anyone else in the room. There had to be a hundred people in here. Sometimes I forgot just how big this organisation was.

Someone sitting at a table at the far end of the room caught my eye, although they were being blocked by someone leaning forward at the table so I couldn't be sure. It wasn't him, was it?

"Our second award is for…"

The person leaned back in their seat again and then I had a perfect view. It was undeniably him, Zack. He looked positively edible. A dark blue dinner jacket and a white shirt, no tie, top buttons undone revealing a little bit of flesh. I couldn't believe it. We were both out at an event together, away from the office. *I wonder if he's seen me. I'm so glad I chose this dress, it shows off my curves in all the right places.* I couldn't take my eyes away from him.

The room suddenly erupted in applause which woke me up from my man coma. I looked back to the stage to see a young man accepting his award. I didn't hear his name, but he looked so familiar.

"Here is your award, sir." Mr Leeming handed the man his award and shook his hand, posing for the photographer who was standing at the side of the stage. "Everyone, once again, Oliver Hallam."

The applause returned, and so did my memory. That was Oliver, from school. I'd not seen him since we left there a million years ago. What a blast from the past. His hair was still a fiery red but he had managed to control the curls. He walked down the stage steps and back to his seat only two tables away from mine.

"Is there anymore Prosecco in that bottle?" Cheryl asked me, pointing in front of Angela.

"Probably but, I don't think she'll let us have any more until this thing is over."

"Damn."

Once all the awards were handed out, we were all free to head to the open bar. It's funny how there is such little funding for our department yet events such as these can be paid for year after year. I would have complained, however, there was good wine available. James would have been impressed at the selection.

I was handed my large Sauvignon Blanc and was about to head back to my table when I saw *him* standing with a group of men from his team. He looked so handsome, and then he spotted me and smiled. Nothing could make my heart flutter like a smile from Zack, especially when it was directed at me. He said something quickly to his colleagues before moving away from them and heading in my direction.

This was it. Do not be a tit. Do not say anything stupid. Do not talk about your cat. Say something nice about him.

Compliment him. He looks great in a suit. It's nice to see him outside the office. Wouldn't it be wonderful to have his babies...?

"Jenny?" Someone from behind tapped me on my shoulder.

"Yes?" I looked behind me and it was Oliver. He had a huge smile on his face. "Oliver, wow, hi."

"I thought it was you." He pulled me in for a hug that lasted longer than necessary. "It's so good to see you! How are you?"

"I'm great, thanks." I looked behind me and Zack had changed his mind about walking in my direction and resumed his conversation with his colleagues. He actually looked disappointed too. Dammit! "How are you doing?"

"I'm good, ta. You look stunning, but then you always did."

"Aw thank you." I was trying to sound sincere, but I was too distracted glancing at Zack, hoping to catch his eye again.

"I didn't know you worked here too. How long have you been here?"

"Oh, quite a while."

"I only started two years ago, I love it..." Oliver carried on talking about himself while I spied on Zack. His group was suddenly joined by several pretty girls. One of them, the prettiest of them all, was talking to Zack. It looked like she was flirting with him. Damn her and her fabulously long legs and tiny waist. She looked like she lived on lettuce and air. "...So, what do you think?"

"I'm sorry?" What was he saying? I hope it was nothing important.

"Catching up properly tomorrow, what do you think?"

"Erm, yeah, sounds great." I had nothing better to do, and thinking back, we were friends in school. It would be nice to talk about the good old days and laugh about all the daft things that happened. "I'll give you my number."

"That's great." I keyed my number into his phone. "Text me with a when and where. I'm free all weekend."

"Will do." He looked very happy with himself. I don't know why though, it was only a catch-up.

"I need to get back to my table," I looked back around for Zack but he'd disappeared. The stick figure tramp was still there though, I'm pleased to say. At least he hadn't gone home with her, although the night was still young. "I'll speak to you later."

I walked back to my table with a bit of a sulk on. I can't believe that Zack was coming over to talk to me, me! He wanted to speak to me, but what about? How would that meeting have gone? Just a friendly chat, or some flirting maybe? I'd never know. Who knows when I would next see him at work.

"Are you all right?" Cheryl asked me. "Who was that guy you were talking to?" Cheryl always loved a bit of gossip. Never tell her anything you want keeping a secret. If I had told her about my crush on Zack then he would know about it by now, as would my boss, my mother and the Mayor of London.

"My friend from school, he won one of the awards. I didn't know he worked here. We were catching up. What time is it?"

"Half past ten. Are you staying much longer?"

"Nah." I couldn't see Zack anywhere. "I think I'm going to get off actually. Do you want to share a taxi?"

"No thanks, my friends are in town somewhere so I'm going to go find them."

"Do you want this wine then?" It seemed a waste to leave it, even if it was free.

"Oo yes, thanks." I handed it over to her. "I'll see you on Monday."

"Yes, good night."

I said goodbye to the rest of my table and walked out of the venue, taking my time hoping I would see Zack in case he was hidden in a corner somewhere out of view, but he was not. At least I had that exciting bit of gossip to tell Sarah. How Zack had seen me and had started to walk towards me. My life was so exciting.

CHAPTER 23

I awoke from a disappointing and dreamless sleep. There was no steamy reunion with Zack to pick up from where we left off. All I could see when I closed my eyes was his smile from the previous night. The smile he had for me. I wonder where he went after Oliver rudely hijacked my once-in-a-lifetime opportunity.

The sun was fighting its way through my bedroom curtains, so I knew it was morning. When I picked up my phone to check the time, I saw I already had a text from Oliver. It wasn't even nine yet.

> Hey you, it was great bumping into you last night! Are you free tonight? Let's meet at Circle Lounge in Halifax for a drink. Is 8 okay? I can't wait to catch up.

>> Hey, yes, how random that we saw each other after all this time. That sounds good, I'll see you tonight.

It might not be a date, but it was still male company on a

Saturday night. I was looking forward to it actually, I needed a break from all these terrible blind dates. Oliver and I were never besties in school, but we were part of the same group of friends. We had a lot of classes together and went to the same house parties. It would be good to catch up. I'll have to tell Sarah when I call her later.

When I finally climbed out of bed, I noticed something odd. There was no sign of Bing. He was always either on my bed or by my bedroom door waiting for me to step out onto the landing, usually so he could walk in front of me to try to trip me up, but I couldn't see him. He must have got up early. He'd make himself known in some way later on.

As I got to the kitchen, I went straight to the bread bin to dig out the crumpets. There were two left. They'd gone out of date the previous day but looked and felt fine so I shoved them in the toaster and flicked on the kettle. My phone started buzzing. My mother. I ignored it. I still hadn't fully forgiven her for setting me up with Rob or signing me up for Rent-A-Womb.

Once my crumpets popped up, all hot and crispy, I lathered them in butter and made my way to the living room with a cuppa and phoned Sarah to fill her in.

"I can't believe it!" she said. "That was your moment!"

"I know." I chomped through my crumpets and wiped the melted butter from my chin, "He probably thought Oliver was chatting me up and decided to forget it. That was probably my only chance. And he looked so gorgeous. He always looks yummy, but last night was extra yummy with a cherry on top."

"At least you had *some* kind of male action, even if it wasn't the right guy. Tell me about Oliver, is he hot?"

"Oliver?" I almost spat tea all over my last crumpet at the notion. "Bloody hell, no. Did I never tell you about him from school?"

"His name sounds familiar, but I can't remember. Was he on that photo you had on the wall when we were at uni?"

"Yes, he was the tall one stood behind me."

"Wait, the ginger one?"

"That's the one, do you remember?"

"Erm, Jenny, do *you* remember?"

"What do you mean?"

"Didn't you used to tell me that he was obsessed with you? Was always hanging around you, asking you out, tried rigging a game of Spin the Bottle to get you to kiss him?"

"Erm…" I *had* forgotten, but it was all coming back to me. The love notes that kept appearing in my locker, the Valentine's cards every year, trying to kiss me at parties, and the jealousy when I got a boyfriend. "It's been over a decade, he will have gotten over all that by now surely. Don't you think?"

"I don't know." She sounded concerned. "How long did he hug you for when he saw you?"

"Oh crap, and I gave him my number. He'll have gotten the wrong idea. I was too distracted thinking about Zack. I was barely even listening to him. He could have been saying anything."

"Is it too late to get out of it?"

"No, I can't cancel. Surely he won't think it's a date. He said he wants to 'catch up', it didn't sound like a romantic request."

"But what if it *is* a date for him?"

We were silent as we thought about my predicament. So much for my date-free weekend.

"Will you have your phone on you tonight?" I asked Sarah.

"Volume's set to high, I'll wait for your 'tea' text."

CHAPTER 24

I decided to keep that night's outfit as casual as possible so that Oliver wouldn't think I was making an effort for him. I wore my dark blue jeggings with my long, baggy grey jumper with silver studs on the shoulders. Nice but not too nice. Also, flat sandals. He wasn't worth the pain of heels. I even put my hair up in a ponytail. If that didn't scream "this is casual!" then I don't know what would.

I arrived at Circle Lounge just after eight to find Oliver waiting for me at the bar.

"You look lovely. I always loved it when you wore your hair up." He greeted me with another over-friendly hug. "What would you like to drink?"

"A white wine please."

He leaned over to the barman and ordered a large white wine and a bottle of Budweiser. I checked out what Oliver was wearing and he was also keeping it casual with his red checked shirt, jeans and red Converse. Surely if he thought it was a date he would have made more of an effort? I think Sarah was trying to worry me, this wasn't a date. Once I realised that, I managed to relax. This would be a nice night.

"Why don't we go sit upstairs out of the way?" he suggested. The bar was starting to get busy but there were always tables available upstairs for those who wanted to sit and chat away from the noise. We made our way up and found one in the corner where it was quiet.

"I can't believe we've both been working at the same company and never knew," I said. "How random is that? It's such a big company though I suppose." I figured shop talk would help steer the conversation away from any risk of flirtation.

"I have a… confession to make. I had a feeling you worked there when I applied for the job. Once I was hired, I typed your name into the database for fun and then it appeared, so I figured I'd see you at some point."

"You searched for my name?" Hmm, weird.

He saw the disturbed look in my eye. "Yeah, just for fun one day. I had a really quiet morning so searched for loads of people."

"Okay." I'm pretty sure that's a data protection breach, but let's walk past this. "Do you speak to anyone else from school?"

"No not anymore. It wasn't my favourite time." He took a long swig of his beer. "Do you still see anyone?"

"No, once we all went to college and then uni we all kind of drifted apart. I guess that's natural."

"You don't still speak to Peter then?"

Peter, my boyfriend from secondary school. We started dating when we were fifteen. He was my first love, first kiss, first everything. He was one of the best-looking guys in our year group, so I couldn't believe it when he asked me out. He didn't like Oliver though as he thought he fancied me and hung around me too much. Peter turned out to be a bit of a wanker in the end, but for that first year together I was besotted with him.

"No, definitely not. Last I heard he was on to this fourth fiancée, third illegitimate child, and had a career selling vapour cigs in shopping centres." I realised how judgemental that sounded. At least he was working and providing for his children, unlike some.

"You had a lucky escape then," Oliver said. "How long did it last?"

"Just over two years, I ended it a week after my eighteenth birthday. He'd started to change the year earlier when he became obsessed with smoking weed and stopped showering. I didn't even get a birthday present. I wasn't important anymore, and he made it... clear."

"How? Did he stop calling you?"

"No, he made it blatantly clear to my face when he told me his friends were more important than me." It gets better. "He told me this as my birthday party ended and we were stood outside waiting for our taxi back to his house. I spent a few days mulling and figured, sod it, he wasn't worth it anymore."

"Wow, what a birthday present."

"Yep, 'happy birthday, I prefer smoking weed with my pals than seeing you', that basically confirmed that we were over, so I decided that was it. He was gutted of course, but it was too late."

"You were too good for him anyway, I always thought so."

"Thank you." I smiled, although this was tinkering very close to date chat. "What did you do after school?"

"Not much. College. Uni. Work. The usual." He took another swig of beer. "So, are you seeing anyone now?"

"Erm, no, not right now. Which uni did you go to?"

"You're available?" He leaned in closer and looked into my eyes a bit too deeply, I could see my stunned expression reflecting back at me in his glasses. I kept my hands out of reach in case he decided to try to hold them romantically.

"Yes." Please don't ask me on a date. Or, a second date, as you clearly intend this to be classed as a first one. "But I'm not wanting to..."

"We could go out sometime then, yes? A proper date?"

"Erm…" I quickly downed the rest of my drink. That was a large glass of wine. "Why don't we have another drink?"

"Yes!" He stood up too quickly, knocking the table with his knees. "I'll go get you one. Same again?"

"Yes, but just a small please." I didn't intend on staying too long.

"I'll be right back."

He shot down the stairs as quickly as Road Runner escaping from Wile E Coyote and out of sight to the bar. I quickly pulled out my phone and typed out "tea" in a message ready to send to Sarah once I saw him walking back. She was right about him. I'd have to endure the "*I told you so*" conversation when I got home.

As soon as I saw his orange head bobbing back up the stairs I hit send and then left my phone on the table. And hoped Sarah didn't let me down again.

"Here you go." The small glass looked fairly large. "I know you said small, but we have loads to catch up on."

"Thank you." I took a sip and within seconds my phone rang. I was saved. "Oh, sorry, that's my friend Sarah. I hope she's okay." I picked up my phone. "Hello?"

"Hello, it's me, your house exploded." She came out with it so quickly and unexpectedly that I had to hold in a laugh. It was a good thing Oliver couldn't hear her over the music.

"Hi, Sarah, are you okay?"

"Bing swallowed a balloon, inflated it as a result of farting and now he's floating down the road. I can't catch him. He's currently racing a Jet2 plane to Amsterdam."

"Oh no, you're kidding." I tried to sound shocked and upset by what she was telling me, but she was making it far too difficult. I had to put my hand over my mouth to hide my smile. "Do you need me to help?"

"I put rocket fuel in my car and now I'm floating around in space because I hit the accelerator instead of the brake."

"Oh my God, I'm on my way, stay where you are." I put my

phone back into my bag, looking up to a very disappointed Oliver. "I'm so sorry, I have to go help my friend." I stood up.

"What's happened? Is she okay?"

"Yes, she erm, she…" Dammit, Sarah has filled my head with funny stories I can't think of anything serious. "She's had a little bump in her car. She's okay but shaken. I'll have to go help her, she's on her own."

"Where is she? I can drive you."

"No! No, you stay and finish your drink, there are taxis outside." I grabbed my jacket. "I'll see you later. Maybe at work sometime. We'll catch up another day."

I turned and ran before he could hug me, impersonating Road Runner myself, and was soon out the door and into the fresh air. I decided not to hang about in case he came looking for me so found a taxi. It was still early evening so there were loads available to take me home.

The taxi had to drive by the bar to go in the direction of my house. I was expecting to see Oliver loitering outside looking like a lost puppy so held my hand over my face to remain as hidden as possible, but it wasn't Oliver I saw outside the bar. I saw Zack, making his way in among a group of friends, looking absolutely gorgeous.

CHAPTER 25

"*I* told you so!" Sarah's voice bellowed down the phone at me. I facetimed her as soon as I walked through the door.

"I know you did." I dropped my keys on the coffee table. "I can't believe it. And I can't believe I forgot what he was like in school. It's my own fault."

I wandered into the kitchen to grab the wine from the fridge. There was enough left for one glass. What I wouldn't have given for James' wine cabinet. It'd be like having my very own Tesco alcohol aisle. Wine on demand which would come in really useful for these situations I seem to find myself in.

"What if I'd been busy tonight and couldn't call you? You'd still be stuck there with him drooling all over you, tricking you into marriage or something... hello? Are you there?"

"Yes, sorry." I was staring at Bing's food bowl and the mound of dry food. "I don't think Bing has been home. His food hasn't been touched. I don't think he was home last night either."

"He's been away for a few days before, hasn't he? He'll be fine."

"Yeah, he'll be back when he's plotted some evil plan to use against me. So," I poured the wine into a glass, "when are you free? I can't believe I haven't seen you for so long!"

"It'll have to be when I get back from my holiday now. We go on Wednesday."

"*I* can't believe you're off to Lanzarote for two weeks. How would Max feel about coming back after a week and I join you for the second week?" Not a totally unreasonable request.

"Ha-ha, I'll let you ask him that."

"Just don't be falling pregnant, you'll ruin my hen do plans."

Her eyes lit up. "Ooh have you booked anything yet?"

"Not yet, but I know what I want to happen. I just need to get the Facebook event page set up so I can get an idea on numbers coming."

"What are you planning?"

"You'll find out on the day!"

"You won't be able to keep it a secret, you'll blab!"

"I'll try my best not to, this has to be a surprise. Anyway," I sipped my wine. I decided to drink it slowly so it would last the rest of my night. "I'm going to go and stick a film on to watch in bed."

"Okay, hun. I'll try to keep in touch while I'm away. I'm happy to be on hand for more emergency calls if you get stuck on a disaster date."

"Without you here to set me up on them, I don't think I'll be out much. Speak soon. Have a good time."

CHAPTER 26

*T*he next few weeks went by rather slowly and boringly. Work was quiet, which was worrying. The general public must have run out of things to complain about. I liked the odd occasional quiet day where I can sneakily read a book at my desk, but without the footfall of customers we have little chance of an increase in funds next year. There was no Zack during this time, so I had to rely on my daydreams in order to see his beautiful face. Cheryl had been on annual leave too, so I had no one to gossip with. I decided to book some time off for myself, so when Friday came along I could relax as I wouldn't be back for ten days.

"What are you doing with your week off?" Angela asked as I was signing out to leave. "Are you going away?"

"No, nothing like that. Just some time to myself really."

"Any signs of your cat yet?"

"No, still nothing." I sighed. Bing had been gone for nearly a month. It was the longest he'd ever been away from home. I was actually missing him which surprised me and thought the worst had happened. My brother had made up some posters for me, which was lovely of him, and we posted them around the neighbourhood. I was surprised he made such an effort for the cat that pushed over his child as it was taking its first steps in my living room.

"He's probably curled up on the lap of an old lady who's taken him in," Angela assured me. "He'll be fine."

"He'll be fine, not sure about the old lady." I put the pen back down on the signing-in book. "I'll see you later."

As I walked out of the building, I was faced with the heat of the September sun. It was still hot and there wasn't a cloud in the sky. I was suddenly in the mood to go to the pub and sit outside with a drink, but I had no one to go with. Sarah was back from her holiday but we couldn't meet up until the next day. We were finally going to see each other after such a long time apart. I hoped she'd brought me a present back from her holiday.

I slipped off my cardigan to try to get some sun on my pasty arms while I walked to my car. I'd made the mistake of parking in the middle of the car park, away from the shade, so my car would be like a furnace when I got inside. I had become acclimatised to the chilly air conditioning in the office so the heat was almost a shock to the system.

Walking through town on a hot day brought out some interesting sights. Just like the rain pulled the worms out of the soil and onto the pavements, the sun pulled out all the chavs. Men, old and young, walked around topless displaying their beer bellies and faded blue tattoos. Women pushed their prams with one hand, with a fag in the other. The kids in the prams munched on sausage rolls, bored as they were being ignored but also flustered from being outside in the heat. I'd only been walking through town for two minutes and it was too hot for me.

My car, as expected, was bloody boiling when I sat in it. I turned on the air conditioning straight away. I was reluctant to open the windows as the last time I did, a wasp almost flew in. I don't need that kind of trauma.

I turned off the radio and plugged in my USB. This kind of

weather was meant for some old school tunes. As soon as I had Good Charlotte's Greatest Hits playing I set off, singing loudly along with the band. My drive home usually lasted roughly forty minutes with the tea-time traffic, so I could get through the entire album.

I had my phone connected to the car via Bluetooth, so when Sarah called it interrupted me as I was singing along to 'Girls and Boys'.

"This better be good," I said as I answered. "You're interrupting some amazing car singing."

"Your windscreen hasn't cracked yet then?"

"Cheeky sod. What you up to?"

"I was calling about tomorrow."

Please don't cancel, I thought. I'd been feeling a bit miserable lately. I'd been looking forward to our lunch date all week. I'd even been checking the menu for La Luna whenever I got the chance to pick out what I was going to eat. The less time I spent looking at the menu, the more time I could spend talking to Sarah. The only people I had spoken face to face with all week were customers, and that doesn't achieve anything more than wanting to bang my head against the wall.

"What about it?" I tried to sound casual, but there was an air of despair in my voice.

"Instead of going for lunch... how about a night out?"

"Really?" We hadn't been on a proper night out in a long time.

"Yes, why the hell not? The evenings are still warm and light, we could have an early bird tea like the old birds we are but then stay out drinking, last man standing, what do you think?"

Times had definitely changed. We never used to eat before a night out, which would explain why, during our student days, we'd have bar staff hoisting us up and off the toilet floor in Rios on a Wednesday night after too many Jägerbombs. One of us would be throwing up and the other half-passed out. Oh, to be eighteen again.

"Oi, less of the 'old', but yeah, I'm up for that!" I turned off the main road and I was getting close to my house. "What time? Where? Give me the details, boss."

"We could still go to La Luna, I'll rearrange the booking, and then take it from there. Go to Circle Lounge, start off classy and with good intentions, but end the night at Cookies like we used to." It's not been a good night unless you ended up in the dive that is Cookies. With its sticky floors, cheap booze and rock music it is the perfect end to a perfect night.

I was suddenly going through my wardrobe in my head, trying to pick an outfit. I'd also need to go back to La Luna's online menu and change my order. I didn't want to feel fat and bloated if we were going out drinking and dancing after eating.

"Let's do it!" My mood was starting to pick up and I felt very giddy for the new plan.

I turned down my road, narrowly missing one of the neighbour's children that decided to run out into the road without looking. The sun was still shining and I could smell barbeques being lit from nearly every garden.

"I'll meet you at La Luna at six, we've loads to catch up on. Right, I'll let you get back to your singing."

"I'm home now anyway." I pulled into my driveway. "The world will need to be deprived of my beautiful voice until next time. I'll see you tomorrow, babe!"

"You will, see you tomorrow!"

That certainly perked up my mood. I grabbed my bag and cardigan off the passenger seat and stepped out of the car. I'd been protected by the cool fans in my little Citroen, I forgot how hot it was outside. There was no wind in my little cul-de-sac, our houses created a barrier against a decent kind of breeze. It would be great for sunbathing, but how often does one wear a bikini in one's own garden?

I hoped Bing was okay. He hated being out when the sun's

shining. The hair on his ears is really thin so his poor ears can burn easily. I tried to put sun cream on them once, you can probably imagine how well that went down. When I walked in, I glanced at his food bowl as I'd been doing every day, it was still full of biscuits.

I stood in the kitchen contemplating what I could have for tea. I was debating ordering a Chinese as a treat. Enough time had now passed for me to get over my flatulence trauma, but I had actually lost over a stone since giving up the greasy goodness. My fridge was no longer filled with half-empty takeaway boxes, but now contained actual food that could be cooked. On Wednesday I'd made a chilli and there was still a small portion left. I decided to stick to my unintentional healthy eating and finish off the chilli. It was surprisingly good and would have been a waste to throw away.

As I was putting it in the microwave, my phone buzzed. It was Dan calling me. I didn't know whether or not to answer. I didn't want him to think I was avoiding him, but at the same time, I was trying to avoid him.

"Hey, gorgeous, long time no speak, how are you?" he said as I answered.

"Hey, I'm fine thanks. How you doing?"

"I'm pretty good, you free tomorrow night?" He sounded very relaxed and casual, more so than me.

"Out with Sarah, sorry."

"That's a shame, I bought a new waterbed and it arrived yesterday. Thought you could come over."

"A waterbed? Are we back in the nineties?"

He laughed. "I've always wanted one, and the nineties were cool. It's really comfy."

"Ha, if you say so, they've never appealed to me much."

"So that's a no for tomorrow then?"

"Can't. Out with Sarah."

"You could come over afterwards? I'll wait up for you."

"No, I haven't seen Sarah for weeks. I don't want to ditch her. Another time, maybe. We'll see."

"Are you avoiding me? I haven't heard from you for ages."

"Not at all, I've been, you know, busy lately."

"Look, you don't need to be embarrassed." Oh, does he really need to bring this up? Even though he's at the other end of the phone, I started to blush. "It happens. We're all human. I farted in the middle of a meeting once. Totally by accident. No one stopped talking about it for months."

"Don't talk about it. Please." I put my other hand over my face as I cringed in the middle of my kitchen floor. "I'm totally mortified."

He laughed again. "Don't be! I won't mention it again, but seriously, I don't care. Come over. What about tonight? I'll be home in a couple of hours. I can send a taxi for you."

"I need an early night, but another time, I will do."

"You'll call me? Promise?"

"I promise."

I wasn't sure if I meant it or not, but as our call ended, I felt happier that we'd spoken and put the farting business behind us. I have my reliable manfriend back. Today has been a very good day. All I needed now was for Bing to reappear. My eye caught something white outside, flying down the road. I ran to out the door to call for Bing but I saw it was just a carrier bag. Where *is* that cat?

CHAPTER 27

Sarah and I were shown to our table by the dashing young waiter. He had olive coloured skin and smelled amazing, like aftershave and pizza. I wanted to tell him, but I'm sober so it would be too weird. That kind of revelation to a stranger can only happen when you've been drinking heavily and can get away with such a creepy comment.

We had been offered a table outside where the sun was still shining, but I hate outside dining. You're just asking for trouble with the wasps. Even though we'd have been under a glass shelter, they'd still be a problem. They seem to be on steroids that year, they never used to be this massive. So, instead, we had a table inside, upstairs on the balcony. It was perfect as it was far enough away from the noise of the kitchen, so we could chat properly.

"Look at your tan!" I said as we picked up the drinks menu. "You look amazing. I look like a milk bottle next to you now."

"But look at how much weight you've lost, it's you who looks amazing! Have you been dieting or something?"

"Kind of, I've not had a takeaway for, I don't know how long. I've actually been cooking."

She put her menu back down on the table to take in the news.

"Wait, you've been cooking? *You* have been cooking? Proper food?"

"Proper food, I'm quite the pro now. I've been making chilli, bolognaise, fajitas. I even made some individual lasagnes to keep in the freezer for when I get home late and I'm too tired to make anything. And I've always got a bowl of salad in the fridge to pick at or have with my tea."

"Wow." She looked genuinely surprised and wiped a fake tear from her eye. "That's so grown up of you. I'm impressed! Are you thinking about hosting a dinner party with James?"

"Ha! Definitely not, but you should come over for tea sometime."

"I think I will. So, why no takeaways? Have you fallen out with them or something?"

"Erm," I still didn't want to tell her, "I fancied a change. I think I was going off it. Do you remember back when I worked at Subway and for a whole year after leaving I couldn't eat one of their sandwiches? I think it's like that. I've had too many. My body wants me to take a break."

"You always looked good, but you look amazing right now. We need some wine to toast."

The waiter came back over as though he had heard her. Dashing and attentive.

"Can I get you ladies something to drink?" He pulled out a device resembling a smartphone and waited for our order.

"Can we get a bottle of the Sauvignon Blanc please?"

"Of course." He tapped the details into the phone. "Would you like some water for the table too?"

"Yes please, thank you."

"No problem at all." He finished his tapping and then headed down the stairs. We watched him walk across to the bar where our drinks were already being prepared.

"What happened to the old days of a pad and paper?"

"I know," Sarah agreed. "Since when did technology take over everything? I still struggle with the concept of streaming music. I don't understand what it means."

"Oh, tell me about it. Did I mention to you about my car?"

"No, what's wrong with it?"

"They don't come with CD players anymore."

"What? How... how do they expect you to play music? Can you only listen to the radio now?"

"I can play music, but I have to put it all on a USB thingy and then plug it in to my car. I had to get my brother to transfer all my CDs onto my laptop and then onto the USB. Don't ask me how he did it, I haven't got a clue."

"Max was telling me to get a new car a while back, he almost talked me into it. You've just talked me out of it."

"You can't get rid of Minnie!" Sarah's Mini, aptly named Minnie, had served her well for almost ten years. It was a gift from her grandparents for her graduation. It was originally red, but they knew she had always wanted a bright yellow car, so they had it sprayed especially for her. Her granddad died the following year so she vowed never to sell it.

"I might have to anyway. I can't take it with me to..." she stopped herself. "It might be time for a change."

"You can't take it where?"

"Where's our wine?" She looked over the balcony and spied our bottle of wine sitting at the end of the bar, waiting to be brought to us.

"Sarah, where are you going that you can't take your car?"

She looked down at her hands on the table, she was fiddling with her napkin trying to avoid my gaze. The diamond on her engagement ring caught the light and was reflecting on her face.

"Max got the news last week," she began, she kept her head down but raised her eyes to look at me. "He's been offered the job in Canada. We're moving there in January."

I was stunned. I had no words. When she'd broke the news

that they may have to move away, I assumed she had meant to London or Newcastle, not another country. I sat back in my seat and looked towards the window, watching people outside wafting a wasp away from their wine. People think I'm paranoid when it comes to wasps, but they're the biggest bullies of the insect world. Many times I have been made to feel like a victim because of a wasp.

"Jenny, say something." Now it was my turn to avoid looking at her. "Please, talk to me."

"I didn't realise the move meant to Canada. And I thought it would have been after the wedding. Next summer. Or the end of summer maybe. And it wasn't final, you didn't think he'd even take the job."

"Because I didn't want to upset you. It's an amazing opportunity, he can't turn it down. And it won't be forever." She reached across the table to put her hand on mine. "We'll be coming back to get married, but he can only return for two weeks maximum, so we'll need to try work that out nearer the time, and I might not be able to come back before then either depending on if I find a job."

"That's scuppered my hen do ideas."

"What had you planned?"

I thought I may as well tell her. "We were going to Rome." I had quickly managed to create a Facebook group and get everyone to agree to the plan.

"Aw, Rome! I've always wanted to go there!"

"I know, but it's fine." I tried to make light of the situation. "We can go another time, just us."

"How much of it had you planned? I hope not too much. Had you spent any money?"

"No," I lied, "I'd only suggested the idea to people and was researching flights for the best prices. That's all."

I'd need to contact everyone on the Facebook group to let

them know the plan was off. I would need to contact the airline to cancel the seats I'd reserved and lose my deposit. I'd need to contact the hotel in Rome to cancel the booking. And I'd need to cancel the time I had booked off work. The latter didn't matter, I suppose.

The waiter finally returned with our wine and poured out two glasses for us, leaving the bottle in a cooler on the table. We hadn't even read the menus yet, so he'd come back shortly to take our order.

"I'm so sorry," Sarah said, picking up her glass. "I didn't know how to tell you. I didn't want to tell you tonight when we were supposed to be out enjoying ourselves. Now it'll have put a damper on the evening."

"It's fine." I picked up my glass too. "I needed to find out some time. Let's make tonight amazeballs." We held out our glasses to each other and they clinked together. "To us."

"To us."

Two huge gulps of wine later, we picked up our menus to choose what we wanted to eat. I was trying to read my menu, but the words weren't registering in my head. I couldn't concentrate. My mind was flipping. I only had three months left with her. I saw the waiter walking back towards our table to take our order, but I still hadn't chosen what I wanted. If Sarah picked something good, then I'd copy her order.

"Have we decided, ladies?"

"Yes," Sarah said, "I'll have the bruschetta to start and fillet of sea bass for my main. Thank you." He tapped her choice into his little device.

"Ooh... that sounds nice. I'll have the same, thanks."

"Very good, thank you ladies." He took our menus from us and walked back down the stairs to the bar.

"I didn't think you liked fish?" Sarah said once the waiter was out of earshot.

"I erm, this diet I've been on, I've been trying new things." She didn't see through my lie. Let's just hope I like sea bass...

"Let's have a good night, yes?" Sarah said. "Please don't think about me moving. Let's talk about you. What have you been up to? Any good gossip?"

CHAPTER 28

"*A* waterbed?" Sarah laughed. "Who has a waterbed anymore?"

"I know!" I filled up our glasses. The food had been amazing. Apparently I like sea bass. We were on our second bottle and trying to get it finished before heading off to find a bar. Thoughts about Sarah leaving me and moving to another country were at the back of my mind, thanks to the wine.

"You need to try it out. I bet it's amazing. When are you going to see him?"

"I don't know, I'm sure I will soon."

"Have you seen much of Zack?"

"Nothing at all." I picked up my spoon to use it as a mirror, I felt as though I had something in my teeth. "He's not been out to our office for ages. His department can't always spare him but I think he works from home most of the time now. I don't know if he's coming back."

"Aw, he will! And you need to make it clear that Oliver was *not* chatting you up, or whatever it looked like he was doing."

"I don't know if I will, I think I'm fed up of trying to get him to notice me. I'm sick of going on dates with weirdos. Can't you just find me a nice Canadian man and I can move over there and live with you?"

"Ha-ha, I'll certainly try! Are we ready to go?"

"Let's finish the wine first, it's good stuff."

We supped the rest of the wine and Sarah put the receipt from our bill in her bag after she insisted on paying. I tried to put up a fight, but she was having none of it, so we compromised, and I would buy our drinks in Circle Lounge.

We said thank you and goodbye to our dashing waiter, and I got one final sniff before we walked out the door and then in the direction of the bar. The sky was clear, but the sun was setting and there was a beautiful haze over the hills in the distance. It was very humid. I was glad I decided not to wear tights with my dress. The extra layer would have been unbearable.

The bar was busy, so we had a bit of a wait before we were served. We decided against any more wine. In our experience, two bottles between us was our limit, so we'd take it easy with some fruit cider. Very little damage could be done with Rekorderlig. Although stranger things had happened.

With our drinks in hand we looked upstairs for a table, but they were all taken, so we found a spot at the bottom of the stairs by the window. The music was loud but we still managed to talk. Conversation had moved on to the wedding.

"And it's going to be so difficult to plan the wedding from another country, so I need to do all I can before we go." Sarah had to shout so I could hear her.

"You can delegate jobs to me though," I shouted back. "If you need me to go to the venue to ask any questions, talk about the food, anything. I can do it. What are you doing about your dress?"

"I spoke to them yesterday, they were so understanding. They've put a priority on my dress order so it *should* arrive before we move. I'll have a fitting or two done then and when I come back before the wedding next year they'll do any final alterations.

But I need to go the day I get back into the country so they have plenty of time to get it done before the actual day."

"That's really nice of them."

"I thought so too. But it means when I get to Canada I can't gain or lose any weight. That'll be six months of being sensible, but not too sensible that I lose anything. It's going to be hard. What if I don't like any food there? Or what if I like it too much and gain loads of weight? Don't they put maple syrup on everything?"

She was starting to flap. Sarah was great at staying calm and keeping things under control, but on the rare occasion she panicked, she would really panic.

"Stay calm, it'll be fine! Don't worry about the wedding, you'll have me on this side of the pond as well as your parents to do anything that needs doing over here. And before you go, ask them to give you your measurements so you can try to come back the same size. Every 'problem' has a solution."

"Who's that?" she asked, looking at the crowd behind me.

"Who?" I looked back but didn't know who she was talking about.

"Him, there. The guy with the light blue shirt. Short-ish, standing next to the guy in the red shirt."

I skimmed the crowd and saw who she was looking at. He looked familiar, but I couldn't remember his name.

"I feel like I know him from somewhere, but I can't remember where, why?"

"He keeps looking over at you. He said something to his friend and then he looked too. Do you know them both?"

I looked again, this time at the guy in red. "Never seen the friend before, but I know the little guy."

As I said that, he looked up and caught my eye. He smiled and waved and I automatically waved back, as you do. Then it came back to me.

"Oh, yes, I used to work with him at that insurance company, before I moved to the council."

That was a very long time ago. I left when I decided I needed a change of scenery, and a better salary. This guy worked in a different department but was friends with a guy, Alex, who took a shine to me. I took a shine to Alex too but was dating someone else at the time. Apparently twenty-year-old me had no problem finding a guy to date.

"What's his name?"

"I really can't remember."

Sarah found this funny, even more so when he and his friend started to walk over to join us. They navigated their way through the crowd and joined us at the bottom of the steps.

"Hi, Jen!" he said, standing a little too close to me. "Long time no see, how are you?"

"Hi..." Finally, it came to me. Better late than never. "Chris! I'm great, thanks. This is my friend Sarah. Sarah, this is Chris, we worked together at Provident."

They exchanged "hellos" and he then introduced his pal as Ryan. The more Chris spoke the more I remembered what he was like back when we worked together. He was friendly enough, but when he heard that my boyfriend and I had broken up not long after I left the company, he used to message me a lot wanting to meet up. He eventually got the hint and I never heard from him again.

He was still standing too close to me.

"So, are you still at Provident?" I asked him.

"No, I left that place years ago. I'm at Direct Line now. It's loads better."

"Ah good."

I glanced at Sarah and gave her the look. The kind of look that's only understood by best friends. The look that said, 'We need to leave now, drink up'.

"Are we getting off soon, Jen?" she asked. "Time to move on I think."

"Oh yes, definitely if you want to."

"Where are you headed now?" Chris asked.

"Erm, we…"

"We're off to Middle Bar," he said. "Do you want to join us?"

"Oh no, we said we'd call in at…" I looked at Sarah, my mind had gone blank. All the bars to choose from in Halifax and I couldn't recall a single one.

"Plummet Line."

"Yeah, Plummet Line. Sorry."

"I've not been there for ages. What do you think, Ryan?"

"Yeah, mate, sound, let's do it," Ryan said, a little too eagerly.

"We'll come with you then." Chris looked too happy and giddy.

"Oh great." I looked at Sarah, giving her a different look. The look that said "bollocks". How are we going to get away from them?

We all walked up the road together, walking past Middle Bar where we should have been losing our two shadows. We crossed the road and found our way to Plummet Line. Sarah and I never went there as it was not on our usual route of places to drink. I didn't realise it was still open. The last time was for the 2010 World Cup final. That was a warm day too.

We walked in together and Sarah pulled on my arm.

"We're nipping to the ladies, we'll meet you at the bar."

"Good stuff, what are you drinking?"

"Get us a bottle of wine, we won't be long."

The men walked to the crowded bar and Sarah pulled me in the direction of the ladies' toilets, which happened to be right next to another exit. I wasn't expecting to be dragged outside. Sarah, not letting go of my arm, pushed open the door and we went straight into the road and quickly made our way back towards town.

"I wonder how long they'll wait for us," Sarah said as we found our way to the Upper George pub. The floor was always sticky in there, but it didn't bother us as they always played great music. This pub had an unusual layout; the circular bar was in the centre of the room so you could be served from any side. There were tables and chairs all around with booths at the far end. It wasn't particularly spacious, but they would sometimes have bands playing. Tables and chairs would be pushed together leaving very little room so sitting would be a struggle. There was no band playing that night though so we happily found somewhere to park our bums.

"I don't care," I said. "Serves them right for thinking they can hijack our night. I mean, who does that?" I put my drink on a coaster, which was unnecessary judging by the state of the table. "Right, so, where were we before being rudely interrupted? Canada. Wedding."

"Yes, are you okay talking about the move? I know I said we wouldn't, but it's all I can think about. I've wanted someone other than Max that I can talk to about it. He doesn't understand."

"It's fine, talk to me. That's what I'm here for."

"I'm anxious about the move. Really anxious. What we can take with us. What we *need* to take with us. What the house will be like over there. Did I mention Max is going over next month?"

"No, what's he going for?"

"They want him to meet the people he'll be working with so he's going for two weeks for a settling in period. They're putting him up in a hotel, but he'll be able to see the house so can tell me what we need. I've told him to take loads of photos so I can see it properly. It's fully furnished which is fab."

"What about your house here?"

"We've still got the mortgage on it. We might rent it out but will wait until after the wedding as we'll need to stay there when we come back. It depends really on how Max's job goes, whether it's a permanent move or temporary as to whether or not we sell up."

"That was your dream house though. It's my dream house. I'd be buying it from you if I could afford it."

"I know, but it's only a house. Bricks and mortar. It's not important."

I wish I could believe her. She'd wanted that house for a long time. She worked so hard and made loads of sacrifices to save up the money for a deposit, they both did. It sits at the bottom of a cul-de-sac with their extension looking over field after field. Every spring there would be lambs sitting only a few feet from us as we'd drink tea sitting on the couch. There were two lounges downstairs and the master bedroom had an en suite and walk-in wardrobe. It was an amazing first house.

I heard my phone bleeping in my bag so pulled it out to see what it was.

"It's Dan," I told Sarah. "He wants me to go over tonight."

"Oh, you should! Go test out that bed!"

"No, this is *our* night out. I told him I couldn't when he called me yesterday."

"What did he say in his message?" She points to my phone.

"Hey babe, my offer still stands for tonight. I'll wait up for you, come and see me."

"You should go, it's only eleven. Give it another hour and we'll head for a taxi."

I was tempted. Plus I was curious about the waterbed and what it would be like to have sex on it.

"You sure you don't mind?" I'd just had a leg and bikini wax. It would be a waste to go unappreciated.

"Not at all!" She fumbled about for her bag. It was then I realised we were both kind of tipsy. "I'll go get us one more drink, text him back that you'll be with him soon. Don't give him a time though, keep him waiting."

"Will do."

She got out of the booth and walked to the bar, so I sent him a message. It took a while to type out as the letters were moving around my phone for some reason. I had to squint to focus on them.

> Okay, woon't be lonb. Gonna have anoher drink and thnn head foor a taxi. Sww you soon X

He quickly replied.

> I'll keep the bed warm for you X

CHAPTER 29

*E*ven at midnight, it was still humid outside. Sarah had pulled the receipt from our meal out of her bag and started using it as a fan. In the taxi I opened the window, hoping to let some fresh air and a breeze in, but there was no wind. The air was still and it was far too warm and sticky. I'd found a hair bobble in the bottom of my bag and had to put my hair up to get it away from my neck as it felt like I was wearing a scarf.

We dropped Sarah off at home and she made me promise to text her when I was in Dan's house, so she knew I was okay. It was not far to Dan's, so it wouldn't take long to get there anyway. Our driver was getting frustrated as our goodbye took quite a while with all the "I love you" declarations to each other.

"Well hello," Dan said as he opened the door.

"I hope you've got a fan on, it's boiling out here."

He nodded. "I left a fan on in my room, so it should be cool. You look amazing."

I smiled. "Thank you." I wasn't seeing two of him which was a good sign.

"No, really, you look good." It was strange to get compliments from Dan. We weren't the complimentary kind of people, it wasn't normal in our relationship. He grabbed my hand, lifted it above my head and twirled me around. "Really good, that's a good dress." He then pulled me in for a kiss. This was far too romantic and alien.

"Have you been drinking too?"

"I had some beers while I was waiting for you. I figured you'd had quite a lot to drink from that last message."

We stood and kissed in his kitchen. His hands wandered around my body. We'd never done this before. Our physical relationship had always been limited to his bedroom. The only thing that ever happened in his kitchen was he cooked a really good breakfast for me after we used each other for sexual pleasure.

"Come on." He pulled me by the hand and led me upstairs. I'd never known him so eager and horny.

We walked into the bedroom which was really warm. It was like being back outside. In fact it was warmer than outside.

"Damn, the fan hasn't been on." He checked the plug and it was all okay. "It must be knackered." He gave it a whack and it started spinning, but not fast enough to be effective.

In the centre of his bedroom was the new king-sized waterbed. It looked like a normal bed. I didn't know what I was expecting as the water was inside the mattress, not in a moat around the bed frame. He had new bedding too and it looked like new pillows. The old ones were almost flat he'd had them for so long.

I kicked off my shoes and began unbuttoning his shirt while he kissed me and held his hands on my face. It was very passionate. And I was pleased to realise that I didn't feel any kind of bloatiness in my tummy.

I pulled off my dress from my sticky body and he slipped out of his trousers. Now was the time to test out the bed.

It's a good thing I don't get motion sickness. As soon as I laid on the bed, I felt like I was on a lilo on the sea. As he climbed on top of me, pushing his hands into the bed above my head, it had a ripple effect on the mattress. I couldn't stop myself going up and down, up and down. We clonked heads as my head involuntarily bounced up as a result.

"Ow, sorry!" I said.

"No, that was me. I think that was me."

He tried to keep up with the movements of my head which was being forced to move by the water in the bed. In the end I put my arms around his neck to try to make things a bit steadier. It did the trick, but his back was damp with sweat. We were finally in unison with each other. That was until we tried to have sex.

He was still on top, but it was not good. I was stuck on the bottom and couldn't move. The only movement from me was when the waves from the water had me bopping like a buoy in the sea. I couldn't match what he was doing. And the more effort he put into moving, the warmer things became. I could see sweat building on his forehead. I was really uncomfortable. It felt like I had an adult-sized hot water bottle on top of me.

His movements slowed down until eventually he stopped.

"Erm, I... erm," he stuttered. "I think I'm too warm."

"It is warm in here, oh," I suddenly understood. I looked down to where our crotches met and amongst all the sweat was a shrivelled, shrunken cock. "It's okay. Don't worry. It's fine."

It really was fine. Waterbeds are not all they're cracked up to be and I wasn't enjoying it. At that particular moment, I would have gotten more pleasure by jumping into a freezing cold bath while eating a big tub of ice cream.

"Damn, that never happens." He pushed himself up and moved to the end of the bed to stand. I bobbed up and down as he took his weight off the mattress. "I'll go get another fan, there's one in the spare room." He pulled on his boxers.

"All right, that's fine."

"Do you want something to drink? I've got plenty of ice in the freezer."

"Just some water, please, with loads of ice."

"Right, I'll be back. We can stick a DVD on or something."

"Sounds great." I smiled. I know a man's ego can be really affected by something like this, but I think we were even now with embarrassing moments. If he ever mentioned the farting again then I'd remind him of this. Thank you, karma.

As he went out in search of the fan and to bring refreshments, I reached for my bag and pulled out my phone. I'd forgotten to text Sarah so had best do that now.

There was a notification in Messenger, someone not on my friends list had sent me a message request. I was tempted to ignore it, thinking it would be Chris asking where we were. I could imagine him still sitting at the bar in Plummet Line with our bottle of wine waiting for us to get back from the toilets.

I clicked on to see the message, it was not Chris.

Hi, how you doing? x

It was Zack.

CHAPTER 30

hat do I do now? Do I reply? What do I reply? Do I wait until morning? Should I speak to Sarah first for help? Should I wait until I'm sober? Can Zack see that I've read the message? Will he think I'm avoiding him if I don't reply? Why does he want to know how I'm doing? He sent it at half eleven, why was he thinking of me so late? Has he messaged me by mistake? What should I do?

Dan walked back in the room with two large glasses of water. "Everything okay?"

"Yeah, fine." I quickly closed down Messenger. "Do you mind if I have a shower? I'm really warm, a cool shower might help."

"Of course, you don't need to ask."

"A quick one, then we can chill out."

"Go for it, I might have one too. I found the other fan so I'll bring that in. I'll fetch you a towel." He placed the glasses on the bedside table and then walked back out on the landing. I heard the floorboards creaking as he made his way to the other room. When he returned, he had the fan and then handed me a clean towel.

"Thank you, I won't be long."

I stood up off the bed and had to stand still for a moment,

suffering slightly from being on the waterbed, although the alcohol could have been partly to blame. I took my phone into the bathroom and opened up Zack's message. I took a screenshot and sent it to Sarah, asking what I should do.

The cold shower was a good idea. My hair was still in a bun so I could let the water trickle around my neck and down my back. It didn't take long to cool down. Once I was finished, I had a reply from Sarah.

> Omg, this is it. The moment you've been waiting for! Typical you're at Dan's though!!! Aaahhhh!! Reply asap so he doesn't think you're ignoring him. Sound casual, don't tell him where you are!

> Really? So he won't want to know I've just come to another man's house for sex? I'll think of something X

I wrapped myself up in the towel and put the toilet lid down, so I had somewhere to sit and concentrate. I reopened Messenger and typed out my reply.

Hey, I'm really good thank you. It's so nice to hear from you X

Simple, but effective. I checked and rechecked my spelling. Predictive text can be mean to you after a few drinks.

I wrapped myself in a towel and made my way back to the bedroom. Dan handed me one of his T-shirts that I could wear to bed and then made his way to the bathroom for his own cold shower. My phone buzzed.

Did you have a good night? I saw you in Plummet Line, but you disappeared x

He was there? I can't believe it!

It was a really good night. We didn't intend on Plummet Line, we needed to ditch some guys who had latched on to us... I didn't see you or I might have stayed X

I pulled off my towel and allowed the fan to blow on my

naked body for a few seconds. There were still some trickles of water on me from the shower. When goosebumps appeared on my arms, I pulled on the T-shirt and slipped my knickers back on.

I was at the bar when I saw you walk in and out. Maybe I could take you for a drink sometime and protect you from uninvited company x

Oh crap. Oh wow. Is this for real?? I could feel my cheeks burning. I thought I was dreaming until I sat on the bed a little too hard and bounced up and down from the waves. Goddam waterbed! I'll be getting seasick soon.

That would be great :) I'd love to X

I had that giddy schoolgirl grin on my face again. I heard Dan switch off the shower. I would need to get rid of this smile before he came back in. It would be unfair on him if he knew I was texting another guy while I was in his bed.

Great, I'll message you properly tomorrow. I'm still out and being dragged to Cookies. Speak soon x

I need to get this smile off my face quickly. I picked up my glass of water and started to drink speedily, until a piece of ice touched one of my front teeth. The pain shot through my gums. That definitely did the trick.

"Ahhh," I said, "dammit."

Dan walked back in and saw my pained face. "Are you all right?"

"Yes, the ice touched my tooth."

I put the glass of water back on the bedside table next to my phone. The pain in my tooth subsided, but the smile was trying to creep its way back on to my face. I couldn't believe Zack had messaged me. And I couldn't believe he was in Plummet Line! I could almost hear Sarah's voice telling me it was fate that we ended up there.

"Jenny? Did you hear me?"

"Hmm? Sorry?" I looked up and Dan was staring at me.

"I said what do you want to watch? I have the new *Family Guy* box set."

"That'll do." I wasn't really bothered. In fact... I felt guilty about being in Dan's bed, as though I was cheating on Zack when we hadn't even been on a date yet. I told myself to stop being so silly.

"Do you want anything to eat? It's not too late to order some food in. Your choice."

"No, thanks. I'm off takeaways at the moment." As true as that statement was, I didn't want to risk another night of farting. Especially not in the waterbed. And I didn't want any "jacuzzi" jokes in the morning.

Dan pulled the duvet off the bed and left it in the corner on the floor. He then pulled out a thin sheet from his wardrobe and threw it over the bed.

"This'll be cooler than the duvet," he said. "Unless you want to be uncovered altogether?"

"The sheet is fine, it's thin so will be perfect. Let me help you."

I picked up one side and helped him spread it evenly over the bed. I caught him looking at me.

"What's up?" I asked.

"Nothing." He looked down at the bed, he looked to be blushing, he must still be warm. "This is nice, that's all."

"Making the bed?"

"Yes, I mean no, this in general. Don't you think?"

"Erm, sure." I had no idea what he was going on about. Nothing about this was nice. It was humid, therefore sticky and horrible. The fans were just blowing warm air around the room. I was starting to get sweaty again. What part of this was nice?

I pulled back the sheet and climbed in, carefully negotiating the waves underneath me. Dan faffed with the DVD and soon an episode of *Family Guy* was playing. It wouldn't be long until I was asleep. My eyes were feeling pretty heavy.

"You do look great, you know. You always do, but you look like you've lost weight."

"Thanks. I've just made a few dietary changes. Nothing too drastic." Not drastic, but I'd had to order in a new work uniform in a smaller size. Knowing my place of work, it wouldn't arrive for another six months when I probably would have put the weight back on.

He climbed into bed next to me. This was usually the point where he lifted his arm for me to snuggle in his nook, but it was too warm for any kind of nooking, as we had just learned the hard way... pun not intended.

We laid next to each other, not touching, trying to feel the breeze from the fans. We each had one blowing on us at full speed, but it wasn't really making a difference.

Then, out of nowhere, something strange happened. Something alien. Something I could never have expected. Dan reached out and held my hand.

I tried not to make a big deal out of it. After all, it's not like I wasn't used to our bodies becoming entwined in one way or another, but hand holding? Fingers wrapped around each other, his thumb gently stroking mine. What the chuff?

I looked up at him, and he smiled at me. There was something different about this smile. This wasn't a "we just had sex" smile or a "I've seen you naked" smile. This was something else.

"Everything okay?" I asked. I didn't know what else to say.

"Fine." He smiled. "Just fine."

Dan soon fell asleep, still holding my hand.

CHAPTER 31

I woke up from a really bad night's sleep. It was a combination of the sticky heat, the rackety fans, the wobbly waterbed, and imagining how a date with Zack might go. Would we go out for dinner and drinks? Would it be to his house for a home-cooked meal? Would he just want to go to McDonald's? Hell, I'd be up for that. It was Zack after all.

Dan eventually let go of my hand once he was asleep, so I could finally turn over to try to get comfy, but I had to move carefully. Every time I moved, the water rippled through the bed and it made Dan move too. I didn't want to wake him up. He might have wanted to hold my hand again.

While wide awake and struggling to sleep, I read over my messages from Zack to make sure it wasn't a drunken dream. The messages were definitely real. Reading them made the butterflies in my belly dance like they'd had too many tequilas.

"Maybe I could take you out sometime." Those would be my new favourite words. I could hear his voice saying them to me. *"Maybe I could take you out sometime."* I just needed to wait for him to message me like he said, so we can arrange our date. Our first date. My first date with Zack. *I'm going on a date with Zack! Eek!*

But, what if he was only texting me because he was drunk? *What if he forgets and never messages me? What if he never messaged me after all and it was one of his friends who got hold of his phone?* Those thoughts were spinning around in my head until I finally fell asleep.

When I woke up, the sun was glaring through the window. The curtains hadn't closed properly as the window had been opened to let some air in, so the room was really bright but it was finally cool. I looked around and Dan was still asleep. It must have been really early. I checked my phone and it was just after eight.

I pulled back the sheet and gently got out of bed, careful not to disturb the mattress too much. The noise from the fans hid the sound of the creaky floorboards as I walked out to the landing and into the bathroom.

When I looked in the mirror, I saw the results of what happens when you mix the humidity and naturally curly hair: a frizzy mess. I didn't have my hairbrush with me so searched through Dan's bathroom for some form of hair taming device. Of course, there wasn't anything in there. I'd need to do the walk of shame looking like the mad scientist.

An unplanned sleepover meant I didn't have my toothbrush either, however I did find some mouthwash during my search for a hairbrush which would have to do. I could have headed straight downstairs from there for a cuppa but I'd left my phone by the bed, dammit!

I quietly walked back into the bedroom, carefully stepping past the fan and leaning across to pick up my phone. My foot, however, decided to get trapped in a wire and pulled the fan off the table. It crashed down onto the hardwood floor, breaking open so the propellers were exposed. Dan jumped and sat bolt upright in bed.

"Sorry!" I cringed. "Sorry, sorry, sorry."

"What happened?" His eyes were wide open with the shock of

the noise.

"My foot got caught in the wire." I looked down at the broken fan. "I really have broken it now."

"Don't worry about it." He got out of bed and walked around to me in my frizzy shame. "It's fine, don't worry. They were only cheap ones from Argos about ten years ago." He stopped and looked at my hair, concerned. "Oh, are you okay? Did you electrocute yourself?" He smirked.

"Sod off." I pushed him away as he chuckled at his own hilarity. "Do you have a brush or something?"

"I don't even think a sweeping brush will sort that out. Let me check, there might be something in the other room."

He then did something. Something even stranger than the handholding. Something I would have bet my life on never happening with Dan. He put his arm around me, pulling me close to him and he kissed me on the head. What was going on with him? It must have been the heat. It was getting to him. His brain must have melted into some kind of mush, leaving him confused. He'd forgotten who I was and why we got together when we did.

"I'll be right back," he said as he walked out of the room, leaving me dumbfounded on the spot. Why had he suddenly started with these gestures? He was being too boyfriendy. I'd never imagined Dan being the romantic type, and certainly not with me. He's not that kind of guy.

I grabbed my phone to check for any messages before Dan returned. There was nothing from Zack yet, but it was first thing in the morning. He could have been in Cookies until the early hours.

"I don't have a brush," Dan called from the other room, "but I do have this…"

I walked out to the landing where I met Dan holding a very mangled comb.

"Why do you have a *comb*?" Combs belong to old men, I don't think I've ever used one.

"I think it's one of those they used to give you at school photo day, so God knows how old it is. But it'll do, won't it?"

"Erm, it might succeed in making me bald but I'll give it a try." I took hold of the comb and watched the dust fly off it.

"You might want to run it under the tap... I'll go get the kettle on."

"Good idea."

"Are you hungry? Do you want the usual?"

"Yes, why not?" I smiled. "I'll be down once I've tackled this." I pointed to my head.

"Okay, there's no rush. I'll see you when you're ready."

Twenty minutes later, I'd managed to regain some of the control of my locks and felt brave enough to make my way downstairs. I was still only wearing Dan's T-shirt so my legs were on show. I was glad they were freshly waxed.

Dan was in the kitchen wearing only his boxers, mixing eggs in a bowl. The sun was beaming through the window behind him. I was pretty sure his teenage neighbour had her eyes on him from her bedroom window opposite.

I stepped towards him when my phone buzzed. It was a message from Zack.

Good morning, hope this doesn't wake you but I couldn't stop thinking about you. Are you still up for going out sometime? x

Oh my God. I had to turn my back to Dan, so he couldn't see my humongous grin. I'm so glad Zack didn't opt for the 'three-day rule'. I don't think I would have coped waiting that long to hear from him. I had to think carefully about my reply.

Hello you, I was awake :) Yes, I'm still up for that. Let me know when's good for you X

He replied immediately.

I'm not sure I can wait until next weekend, are you free one night this week? x

I'm off work all week and no plans made yet, so anytime is good for me X

I could see he was typing his response. I was giddy with anticipation.

How's Wednesday for you? Have you been to Verona's? x

No never, but I hear it's really nice. Let me know what time and I'll be there :) X

I'll call them today and let you know, can't wait x

I couldn't think of anywhere more perfect for a first date. Verona's had a really good reputation but I'd never been able to get in, it was always so busy. I hope he managed to book it. What a great place to suggest. I'd have to avoid my usual steak option, I couldn't be having meat stuck in my teeth again. Unless I took some floss to use before we left. But then what if he kissed me and could taste the mint from the floss? I wouldn't have steak. Or meat. Or anything that could get stuck in my teeth. I'd check the menu and pre-order in my mind in preparation.

"Do you want eggy bread?" Dan's question brought me back down to earth. "Why are you hugging your phone?" he asked as I turned round.

I looked down and was in fact hugging my phone. Clearly my subconscious thought my phone was Zack and placed it conveniently between my breasts for a boob hug.

"Oh, nothing, erm, eggy bread sounds good."

I walked into the kitchen and decided to help out. On the counter behind him were two cups which I presumed were put there for our drinks. I switched on the kettle and decided to get them made as Dan was busy making the food. Or I thought he was busy. Suddenly, I could feel one hand as on my waist as he nuzzled his nose on my neck. He slowly kissed my neck, using his other hand to navigate its way to my front and up my T-shirt to fondle the ladies. Usually, this would have been welcomed with open legs. That morning, however, I only had one thing on my mind. And it wasn't the thing poking into my back. It seemed to have recovered well from the previous night's disaster.

"What are you doing?" I tried to sound playful.

"What do you think?"

He tried to pull my T-shirt up, but I had to stop him.

"No, not now."

He spun me round and with his hands on my hips, he pulled me in to kiss him but I pulled back.

"What's the matter?"

"Nothing, I'm just not in the mood now."

He winked. "I can get you in the mood."

He lifted my arms and put them around his neck, his hands working their way down my body. I felt so guilty, but it didn't feel right anymore to have sex with him. How could I stop it though without offending him? His ego would surely be bruised from the previous night already without me turning him down.

"Look, we can't. The window's open. Someone will see or hear."

This seemed to work. He pulled back and looked at the window, spying his teenage neighbour watching us from her room.

"You're right, we can go back upstairs. Sod breakfast. We can save it until lunch."

"Erm, no, it's still too warm, don't you think? And, I have to be honest, that waterbed is bloody awful."

"Ha-ha! It's going to take some practise. But we can work on it. We've got all day. There's always the couch."

"Actually, I can't stay. I have some things I need to–"

"Jenny, what's going on?" He stepped back but kept hold of my hands. "You're never this distant with me. Are you okay?"

"I'm fine." That was probably higher pitched than it needed to be.

"You can tell me, I'll understand. Was last night that awful? Have I put you off?"

"No, I'm sorry, it's nothing to do with last night." I walked to the dining table and sat down. "I have a thing on Wednesday, it's been arranged this morning. It's a date, but one that I'm actually looking forward to. So, doing this now seems weird."

"Ah, a date." He came and sat next to me. "Not a blind date then? Someone you actually like?"

"Yes, quite a lot."

"Is this the office guy you mentioned a while back?"

"It is, he saw me out last night but I didn't see him, but he messaged me late last night. And he wants to take me out."

Dan smiled. "That's great. I'm happy for you. I hope it works out."

"Thank you, I hope so too."

"Do you still want breakfast?"

"Do you even have to ask?"

He laughed and returned to mixing his eggs in the kitchen as my phone buzzed. It was a withheld number calling me. Who needs to ring me this early on a Sunday morning?

"Hello?"

"Hello, can I speak to Jennifer please?"

"Speaking." I spoke in a monotone voice, expecting it to be a nuisance call about the "accident" I had been in while making a PPI claim.

"Jennifer, this is Gale from Moorside Vets in Huddersfield. We've had a cat brought to us and when checked for a microchip it's come up with your details. Are you missing a cat?"

"I am! Bing!" I stood up in a panic and tears came from nowhere, filling my eyes. "Is he okay? Is he alive?"

I soon discovered that I had feelings for the arsehole cat after all. I couldn't hold back tears as I had visions of Bing being hit and killed by a car, mauled by a dog, attacked by vicious youths with crossbows. Dan was suddenly in front of me, anxiously waiting for news.

"He's fine. Absolutely fine. How long has he been missing?"

"Oh, weeks. A couple of months? I'm not sure now, it's been ages. Is he really okay? Can I come get him?"

"He's alive and okay. We had him in the van and that's when I checked for a microchip. However, when we tried to carry him into the cage, he bit my colleague who dropped him and he ran back out the door." The stupid cat. "I chased after him, but I lost him up one of the side streets. I'm so, so sorry." She sounded like she was going to cry too. "But when I saw your address and how far away you are, I figured you'd want to know where he was in case you wanted to come and look for him."

"I don't know Huddersfield at all but…" I smiled at Dan who was quietly asking if I wanted him to take me there. "Was he thin and hungry? What was he like?"

"There were no obvious signs of malnourishment or cuts from being in fights. He looked perfectly healthy. I'll be back out this afternoon to try to find him but I had to call you first."

"Thank you, I really appreciate you calling me. I'll see you soon."

"Thank you, Jennifer."

We ended the call and I relayed the information to Dan.

"At least you know he's okay. It sounds like he's been looking after himself. But how the hell did he get to Huddersfield from your house? It's about twenty miles away!"

"No idea, he probably manipulated a bus driver to take him. That cat has skills."

"It's still early. Let's have a quick breakfast, then I'll take you home to get changed and we can drive over to try to find him."

"Are you sure?"

"Absolutely. Come on, let's get dressed and then we're ready to go once we've eaten."

CHAPTER 32

*W*e found the veterinary surgery in Huddersfield, thanks to trusty Google Maps, and then walked around the nearby streets for a couple of hours, showing a photo of Bing to random people walking by, but to no avail. A cat as white as Bing stands out like a clown at a funeral, and he had truly made his escape and is out on his own again. At least I knew he was alive after all this time.

That pain-in-the-arse cat clearly had some survival skills. All those nights he howled and howled at me from the kitchen, dragging me out of bed, because his food dish was half empty and he couldn't cope with such low levels of dry biscuits. What a manipulative beast. I can't believe he made it all the way to Huddersfield. He must have hijacked a bus at claw-point and forced the poor driver to take him there.

Dan drove me home in a painfully awkward silence.

"Thank you for taking me to look for Bing, I really appreciate it." We had finally pulled up outside my house.

"It's no problem." He kept one hand on the steering wheel and the other on his lap, not looking at me.

"Okay, thank you again and I'll see you soon." I reached to open the door.

"I'm happy you've finally got the date you wanted, no more awkward, nightmarish blind dates," he said suddenly. "I think my timing was a little off, or too late really."

I put my hand on his and he finally looked me in the eye.

"I'm sorry. I really am. As soon as I got his messages last night I—"

"It's fine, you don't need to explain. I remember you telling me ages ago how much you liked him. To be honest, I should have been more open about my feelings for you. I've just never been a relationship kind of guy, or at least I never thought I was."

"If you want some advice, never let a friend set you up on a blind date. You'll live to regret it."

That made him laugh, finally. I hated seeing him so gloomy.

"Who knows? We might see each other again." He looked at me and smiled. It was a sad smile.

I leaned over and gave him a kiss. A goodbye kiss.

"Another bit of advice, buy a normal bed. No girl will hang around for seasick-inducing sex."

"There's nothing wrong with that mattress! I'm telling you, it will be amazing."

"From a woman's point of view, it really won't." One final kiss on his cheek and then I opened the car door. "You take care."

"You too, Jenny."

Walking into my house, I had a little spring in my step that I felt had been missing for some time. I was suddenly feeling very good about myself. Men are like buses, you spend ages waiting for one and then all of a sudden, two turn up wanting to take things further with you. And then the one man currently in your life clearly hops on one for a holiday away in the next town.

I saw Bing's food and water bowls on the kitchen floor. They were caked in dust, so I picked them up and put them in the dishwasher in case he did end up coming home soon. Think positive.

I decided Sarah would need to be updated with the day's events so pulled my phone out of my pocket, but instead was treated to a text from Zack.

> Verona's booked for 7.30 weds eve, I'll come
> pick you up if you like. Text me your address x

Oh my God, oh my God, oh my God. It's really happening. This is what I'd been working towards with my year of bad blind dates. From questionable Italian food with Gerard, disappointing sex with James, and Dan, fearing for my life with Rob, potentially harvesting my ovaries and an over-obsessive old school friend, it was my turn for some good luck. *I already know that I like Zack, I already know I will love the food, this'll be the perfect date, right?* What could go wrong?

Conversation.

What if we have nothing to talk about? What if he turns out to be really boring? We've always got on in a work environment but that was never constant conversation with each other. It was always more small talk in between jobs. What if he has some strange habits or collects weird objects? Like me with the gingerbread man he bought for me which has been wrapped in cling film and kept in my bedside table all this time. Maybe I won't mention that to him.

I replied with my address and told him I was really looking forward to our date and then phoned Sarah to fill her in. She couldn't believe Dan's behaviour but was excited that my date was finalised with Zack, however, she didn't seem her usual giddy self.

"Is everything okay?" I asked. "You seem a bit off."

"I'm fine, just tired. Had a bit of a migraine that's all. Could be a hangover from last night mixed with the heat. I'm possibly dehydrated. So, what else are you up to this week?"

"Not much, I might go shopping tomorrow for something to wear Wednesday night and wait for another phone call from the vets to tell me they've recaptured Bing. Otherwise, I'm going to chill and take it easy I think."

"That sounds good. Have you got an outfit for Wednesday night?"

She wasn't paying attention. Something wasn't right.

"No, I said I'm going to go shopping tomorrow to get an outfit, are you sure you're okay?"

"Yes, sorry, it's this migraine. I'm going to have to go, I think I need to sleep. Send me photos of your outfit won't you."

"Course I will, I hope I find something. Text me if you need me for anything."

"I will do, speak to you later."

"Bye."

I hung around my kitchen and wondered what I could have for tea. I missed my Chinese takeaways, but all that oil, salt and grease would leave me crippled with a tummy ache. My body couldn't handle it anymore. I'd tried a takeaway pizza a couple of weeks earlier and Imodium was needed at three in the morning. I'd have to play it safe and have a tuna toastie.

I didn't know what was wrong with Sarah, but it was *not* a migraine. I'd ring her in the morning and get her to spill.

CHAPTER 33

*J*love shopping in Halifax. I could spend an entire day walking around the town centre, being mindful of the cobbles of course. Even in my flat sandals, they need to be carefully navigated to avoid disaster. This was not the week I wanted to break my ankle. Any other week but this one.

Starting at the very bottom of town, I went into New Look first. A very well-designed store and always my favourite for clothes shopping, they covered all bases for your occasion. The layout was perfect for whatever you were after. You want glitz and glamour? That would be on your left as you can see. The smart, office look? Still on your left but further down nearer the back, you can't miss it. You're after a new jacket or coat? Of course, they are located in the middle for your convenience. Something a bit more comfortable to lounge around in? There, on your right, row upon row of vest tops and T-shirts in every colour imaginable. Oh, you're after shoes today? Why didn't you say so? Up the stairs on your left and you will be in "Shoe Heaven".

Now onto my dilemma. I definitely wanted to try out new shoes, but I couldn't even think about looking at shoes until I knew what outfit I wanted to wear. And I had absolutely no idea what I wanted to wear. I couldn't even rely on anything in my wardrobe at home because most things were too big for me. A good thing, yes, I felt amazing, but not much help when I needed a decent, reliable outfit. Argh! Did I want to wear a dress? Or trousers? Or a bikini?

I decided the best place to start was on the left. The smart section. I really want to look smart, but nicely smart, like pretty but not too stuffy like I walked out of an executive meeting in a big office. Date, prettily smart. That's a look, right?

There were dresses of all kinds of shapes and materials. Pinafore, skater, wrap, shirt, midi, smock, pleated... the list was endless. Although my eye did immediately catch a beautiful green floral wrap dress. That would pull in perfectly at my waist. It was a V neck too so should show off a respectable amount of cleavage without being too much. The front of the dress looked as though it would reach my knees but then the back was longer. *Yes, love it. Grab it. I'll be trying that one on.*

There were skirts too and I found a really nice red tartan one which would go great with a white blouse I had at home which I already knew still fitted. I'd try that one on too. Trousers might be too formal for a date, however this pair of blue checkered pants would look really nice with a black vest top. There were some summery harem pants too. *What the hell. Let's get to the changing room.*

The dress was gorgeous. Such a nice fit. I wouldn't need much of a heel either, flat shoes would be fine which was always a bonus. The skirt was quite cute too. High waisted so it was really flattering. The trousers, surprisingly, were a little too big. The shop assistant kindly went to fetch me a size ten to try on. I couldn't remember the last time I wore anything in a size ten, but they fitted me. Just.

They weren't uncomfortable at all, a little elasticated in the back which would help after a meal. It might be time to go through my entire wardrobe and have a clear out as there are a lot of size fourteen clothes I'll no longer be needing if I keep this up. Don't you wish there was a place you could exchange your existing clothes and have them replaced with the exact same but in a better fitting size?

I couldn't pick from any of the things I tried on so decided to buy them all. What the hell. It was my week off and I deserved a treat. Plus, as I'd not been buying any takeaways, I had some extra money just sitting in my account. It needed spending.

"This dress is lovely," the young girl serving me said as she scanned and bagged my clothes. "I want one myself."

"It *is* really nice." I smiled. That one may be the winner.

After New Look, I decided perfume was the key, so off up to Boots I went. As I walked up, I went by Costa and the traumatic memory of Rob and his band of merry dead pocket mice came back. Even out in the fresh air I could smell him and it sent a shiver down my spine. I rooted in my handbag for my sanitizer which I always carried around with me since, just in case. By the time I'd squeezed and rubbed some gel into my hands I made my way through the entrance of Boots and walked around to the perfume section.

"Can I help you?" an older lady asked me.

"Yes, please, I'm after something new but I've no idea where to start," I admitted. I really didn't know anything when it came to perfume except they seem to get more and more expensive each year.

"Okay well, I can certainly help you there." She smiled. "What have you had in the past?"

"I currently have Paco Rabanne." I've had this fifty-millilitre bottle for years. I've been using it sparingly for such a long time, making it last as long as possible. Apparently, hinting about it to your family every birthday and Christmas doesn't work.

"So would you say you prefer one a bit more floral?"

"Yes," I lied. I honestly have no idea what I like. "I guess so."

"Okay, let's try a few."

The keys to the cabinets jangled as she picked out several, spraying them on little pieces of thin stripped paper and passing them to me. There were some really lovely ones. Also some really sour ones. One of them however I kept returning to.

"This one." I handed it to her. "Can you remember which this one was?"

She sniffed it and moved a few cabinets down. "Ah yes. It's 'My Way' by Giorgio Armani. I have it myself. It's very popular."

I took a look at the price and almost winced, disguising it with one of the sour perfume samples in my hand.

"Are you wanting it for everyday use? Or is this a special occasion? Because, in my opinion, this perfume is perfect for those one-of-a-kind occasions where you want to stand out."

It was for a special occasion. I wouldn't be wearing it every day. Not unless I was given a perfume allowance at work. I wasn't sure even my uniform allowance would stretch this far. Also, this was a very special date. I hardly ever treated myself. Why was I resisting?

"There is an event I have in mind to wear it at," I admitted.

"I'd suggest buying the smaller size bottle. You won't need the larger one if you won't be wearing it every day. I only ever bring mine out if there's a wedding or party to go to." She winked. "Or perhaps you're looking for something special for a special guy? Either way, I think you can't go wrong with this one."

Zack always smelled so good, why couldn't I smell good too? We could be the extra-nice-smelling power couple.

With my bags full of clothes, shoes, overly expensive better-be-worth-it perfume, I needed a coffee. Costa wasn't even an option, so I walked into The Piece Hall. Walking around the square structure, up and down the stone stairs, was out of the question with all these bags weighing me down so I stuck to the ground level and went into the deli. All the seats indoors were taken, which didn't bother me. The September heat was still lingering slightly so I sat outside in the shade and just ordered an Americano.

Hey, how are you doing? X

I texted to Sarah as soon as I sat down, but there was no reply. She could be busy at work at the best of times, but I guessed she would be building up to finishing there for good soon so would be busy in meetings, making sure all clients were set up for the new year for whoever took over from her.

I couldn't imagine moving to another country. I'm not sure I'd want to move for anyone else anyway. Max is a good guy though. No, he's the best. The kindest and most caring guy Sarah had ever been with. She was elated when he proposed. I've never seen a happier, more suited couple.

Once I finished my coffee I wandered on to The Yorkshire Soap Company in the corner and bought myself a new bar of soap for the bathroom and some reed diffusers for the hallway. The smell always stretched through the entire house which is amazing. Also, it made my mother retch if it was too strong. Especially when she came over the day Bing knocked it off the cabinet causing all the liquid to sink into the carpet. My house smelled beautiful, but my mother refused to visit for several weeks. I missed that cat.

Once fully caffeinated and rested, it was time to go home and hang up my new purchases ready for Wednesday, eek!

CHAPTER 34

ednesday came round all too quickly and I had nothing to wear. Everything I bought on my shopping spree looks stupid on me. The skirt made me look like a frump, the trousers far too tight which wouldn't work for going out to eat. The dress too flowy; I'd be at risk of a Marilyn Monroe moment. My hair wouldn't behave. My eye kept watering, so I needed to keep redoing my make-up. What the hell was going on? Almost half past six, I needed to be ready but I wasn't. I texted Sarah.

> I'm not going. Forget it. I'm cancelling. I can't go. Who needs a man anyway? I've survived being single all this time. I'll live.

Don't you dare cancel! Stop being stupid! I could hear Sarah shouting at me from her text message.

You'll look fabulous, you're just nervous. Wear the dress, that was my favourite and it shows your figure. Zack won't care if a strand of hair is out of place. And men never notice make-up. Stop being a spoon and have a glass of wine while you wait!! Take a deep breath. Chill Xxx

I followed her advice and took a deep breath before putting the dress back on. With a pair of glossy, skin-coloured tights and my white kitten heeled sandals, I actually looked okay. Once I put a smile on too, I felt ready, forgetting the make-up fiasco earlier. Contouring is not for everyone. What should have been accentuated cheekbones and big dark eyes turned out looking like twelve rounds with Mike Tyson. If I hadn't figured out how to apply make-up by then, I never would. Foundation, blusher, mascara, done! No need for messing about like all those Influencers taking over my Instagram reels.

That morning I'd had a glance at the menu on the Verona's website and already picked what I was going to have. All were safe options so no dental floss would be needed. I would also be making sure I had a glass of water on the table at all times to sip in between the wine so I wouldn't get too tipsy and embarrass myself. The night has to be perfect. It will be perfect. I look perfect. He will look perfect. Happy vibes. Happy, not panicky, non-bloaty, totally confident vibes.

My phone buzzed from behind me on my dressing table. It was a text from Zack. My heart pounded as my internal organs tried to make an escape out my arse. I'd need to take some Imodium before I go anywhere.

I think I'm here x his text message read. I glanced out my window and there he was getting out of his blue Ford Fiesta. *I can't believe he is outside my house. Oh, the tingles.*

Crap. Shit. Balls. Do I look okay?

As I did one final twirl in the mirror to check for ladders in the tights and cat hair on my bum, I luckily saw the tag still attached to my dress, so I quickly yanked it off. There will be no embarrassments or disasters tonight, none! I did one final spritz of perfume for good luck, picked up my bag and I was ready…

"Hello there," Zack said as I opened the door. "Wow, you look beautiful."

"Thank you." I blushed, dammit! "You look good too. I'm glad you found my house okay." I stepped outside and we walked side by side to his car. We were so close our arms were almost touching. I could smell his aftershave. I wanted to lick his face.

"I did drive down the wrong street first but I blame the satnav on my phone. Oh, here you go." He walked round to the passenger side and opened the door for me.

I smiled. "Thank you, very chivalrous of you."

"I need to impress you so you have something juicy to tell your girlfriends about me."

"I'll add it to the list. You've got your work cut out though. I hope you're prepared."

"It's a good thing I like a challenge."

He winked as he closed the door and the giddy schoolgirl grin returned to my face. I had to fight to get rid of it before he got in the car.

🖎

Verona's was very busy. I imagine it didn't need to be a weekend for this restaurant to be fully booked. When it first opened, Sarah spent weeks trying to book a table for us until she finally gave in. The heat from the bustling kitchen hit us as soon as the door was opened and the sound of happy chatter filled our ears. The flame from a pan whooshed out of the corner of my eye and perfectly presented meals were placed on the counter ready to be taken to their tables.

The hostess greeted us at the glass door with her picture-perfect smile. Her hair was immaculately presented in a bun without a strand of hair out of place and her make-up looked amazing. How come some people possess the skill to put that amount of make-up on without looking like The Joker's evil twin?

We were taken to a table by the window and thanked the hostess who handed us our menus. I don't think I've ever sat this close to Zack before. We've sat next to each other at work but sitting opposite him was a new experience. Now I didn't need to worry if he caught me looking at him because we were on a date. I was allowed to look at him without it being weird. Eek!

"I hope you're not one of those girls who orders a salad with a side of salad."

"Hell no, I expect the food here will be too good to waste on a bowl of lettuce. I know exactly what I want."

"That's good to know. I had a sneaky look at the menu online earlier so I've already picked what *I* want. Is that weird?"

"Ha-ha, no. I did the same thing. I don't even need to look at the menu."

We put our menus back down on the table. Now for the complicated part of the date: conversation. *What do we talk about?* Years ago, I read that the best way to get a guy's interest is to ask them questions about themselves. Guys love to talk about themselves and love it when girls act really interested. So here goes.

"So how long have you worked for the council?" I asked.

Yes, let's talk about work. Great idea, Jenny.

"Quite a while now, it was my first job straight out of uni. How about you?"

"Too long. I've had a few jobs over the years but seem to have settled there for some reason."

"Where did you work before?"

Conversation was supposed to be about Zack, I'll try to flip it around later.

"My favourite was at the Alhambra Theatre in Bradford."

"Oh wow, were you backstage mingling with the stars?" He placed both his arms on the table so he could lean in towards me.

"No, nothing as exciting as that. I worked on the bar as a supervisor. I loved it. Every now and then I'd spot a star and act like a crazed fan if they spoke to me. Stephen Mulhern was there once to support his girlfriend in a show. He came to the bar and ordered a glass of wine and a bottle of water before I'd even realised who he was. The first words out of my mouth were 'oh wow'!"

Zack found this really funny. A good sign. "What did he do then?"

"Nothing, he looked at me like I was a crazy person and I served him his drinks. He was really nice actually. Also taller than he looks on TV."

"An interesting fact. Which other celebs have you seen?"

"Oh loads. Ainsley Harriot, he was hilarious. Linda Bellingham was my all-time favourite celeb. There was Jimmy Carr, Alan Carr too." His eyes lit up at the mention of all the celebrities I had encountered. "The singing kid too, what's his name, Ray Quinn? Oh, and Connie Fisher! That was a random encounter. She got lost backstage and ended up in the private members' bar area. I think she was as shocked to see me as I was to see her!"

"That sounds really exciting, why did you leave?"

"It was only part-time whilst I worked through university, and by then I needed a full-time job. Some weeks there were no shifts available, it depended on which shows were on. But it will always be the best place I ever worked."

I then noticed a change in Zack's smile. It was the same, but different. Like he was genuinely interested and touched by me recalling happy memories of years gone by. He's never given me that look before. I don't think any man has. I couldn't take my eyes off him, or the smile off my face. I could have slapped the waitress who dared to interrupt us.

"Would you like any drinks?" she asked, looking at Zack.

Damn you.

"Yes, please, erm, a bottle of Peroni, thanks."

The waitress looked to me, but I'd been distracted by my phone buzzing in my bag. I pulled it out and saw it was the vets ringing me again.

"Erm, I, erm." I looked from the waitress to Zack and back to the waitress. "I'm really sorry but I need to take this."

"That's okay, I'll come back in a couple of minutes."

"Is that okay? It's about my cat." Coming across as that crazy cat lady like I warned Sarah I would.

"Of course, go for it."

I answered the call. "Hello?"

"Hi is that Jennifer? This is Gale, we've found Bing again and we've got him! He's in a cage, he's not going anywhere this time."

"He's there? Really?"

"Yes really. He's here and he's a little angry, he's got some vocals on him, hasn't he? But he's absolutely fine."

"Oh, thank you. I'll be there in the morning to get him. Thank you so much."

"Actually, that's why I'm calling you. The surgery is closed tomorrow and not open again until Monday as the veterinary staff are on a training course. There won't be anyone who can look after him. Can you get him tonight? I can wait here until you do."

"Tonight?" I looked up at Zack who was having a look through the menu.

"Yes. I could call the RSPCA to see if they could take him for the night but—"

"No, no don't call the RSPCA," I said as Zack looked up. "I'll come get him tonight. I'll come now. Thank you, I'll see you soon." I put my phone back in my bag.

"Is everything okay?" he asked.

"I'm so sorry. I hate to do this. But my cat. They've found him.

He's in Huddersfield and I need to go get him. I can't believe I have to do this, but I need to get him home."

Zack was going to think this was a lie. Like I had asked a friend to phone me with a ridiculous excuse to get out of the date. He'll never want to see me again. Damn you, Bing, you ruin everything!

"Hey, don't worry about it. It's great that they've found him." Zack put his menu back down. "Come on, I'll take you."

"You will?"

"Yes, it's too late to be traipsing to Huddersfield on your own. Do you need to pick up a cat carrier for him?"

"I'd best do. He's known to be a flight risk." The last thing I needed to be doing in this dress was running around the streets of Huddersfield chasing Bing.

Zack stood. "Come on." He held out his hand to me, which I happily grabbed. "We'll go get the carrier from your house and then we can rescue your cat."

I couldn't believe his reaction. He seemed genuinely concerned. I wasn't used to men being so caring. I couldn't wait to tell Sarah about the twist in our date.

"Thank you, that's so nice of you. I'll warn you though, he won't be grateful, he's kind of a wanker."

Zack laughed. "That's fine. I can cope with that. Small baby steps and I might win his approval at some point."

The waitress came back to our table, seeing that we were leaving.

"Is everything all right?"

"We have an emergency and need to go," he said to her, "but thank you."

He grabbed my hand and led us out of the restaurant and back to his car. Disaster or not, this was my favourite date ever.

CHAPTER 35

"*I*t's up on the left here." I directed Zack via the satnav on my phone. He pulled up in front of the surgery.

"Do you want me to come in with you?" He unbuckled his seat belt.

"I don't know, he doesn't react well to strangers." He didn't often react well to me, but I had horrifying visions of Zack's perfect face being scarred by psycho cat scratches. Then I'd have to kill the cat, and that would mean all the weeks being worried about him would have been a waste of emotion, never mind a waste of a date.

"I'll wait in the reception area then. Come on, I'll take the carrier in for you."

We got out of the car and Zack collected the carrier from the back seat. I suddenly felt nervous. I'd not seen Bing for some time. Would he be excited to see me? Would he even care? Would he have forgotten about me? Was he trying to get away from me? Would he think I'd abandoned him? He was a rescue cat after all, I wasn't the first owner he had to forget about. And cats aren't exactly loyal creatures. I'd read recently that a cat's meow was created by them to get our attention and get their own way. How often do you hear a cat meowing to another cat like a dog barks at other dogs? Yet, they're perfectly able to meow at you. They're sneaky buggers.

Zack seemed to sense my apprehension and he grabbed hold of my hand as we walked to the door. This was a very welcome distraction. I just hoped my hands weren't too sweaty.

We were met at the door by a short plump woman. Her grey roots were peeking out through her faded red hair and her glasses were hanging from her neck on a badly crocheted cord.

"Hi, I'm Gale. Are you Jennifer?"

"Yes, it's me. This is my, erm, my friend Zack. He gave me a lift. Is Bing still here?"

"He's here." She held the door open as we entered the reception area. "He's had some food but he's not a happy chappy! I think he wants his own bed. He's quite a character!"

That's one way to put it. I think he wants to strangle you with that glasses cord for putting him in a cage though.

"Oh, well, his presence has certainly been missed at home." I'd not had to check my shoes before putting them on for spider corpses. Life had been a lot less stressful.

"It's this way."

She walked behind the reception counter and motioned for me to follow her down the corridor.

Zack passed me the carrier and gave me a reassuring smile. "I'll wait right here."

"Thank you."

I followed Gale down the corridor and into a room filled with cages and the blinding smell of disinfectant. There were cages of all sizes. Some were small enough for rabbits and some big enough for a Great Dane. And then there was one with a white ball of fluff in the corner, making a strange sound. A deep, angry growl.

Gale sensibly stayed by the door. "I'll wait out in the reception area." She slowly backed away. "I'll let you calm him and bring him out."

This was going to hurt.

"Bing?" I took a step closer to the cage. "Bing? Here, kitty." Like that ever worked.

Two ears popped up through the fur and the growling stopped. Had he recognised my voice?

"Bing? It's me. Hey, boy."

Two eyes suddenly opened, staring straight at me. The deep annoyed growl suddenly became a high-pitched mew. I'd never heard him make that sound before. Mew. He did it again. And again. He rubbed his head against the cage causing a clattering sound. He wanted to get out. I felt a little emotional.

"Okay, it's okay, Bing. I'm here." I put my hand against the cage and he pushed his head against it.

I made sure the carrier was ready and that the door behind me was shut. I couldn't let Zack witness me chasing Bing around the surgery. I slowly lifted the handle to the cage and pulled it back, gradually pulling the door open until Bing and I were face to face. He couldn't keep still. He seemed jitterish, nervous, excited. As soon as he could, he leapt out of the cage and into my arms. My new dress was caked in white hair, but I didn't care.

"Hey, little man!" I held on to my cat with very little effort to keep him from escaping. He actually seemed happy to be in my arms and purred into my neck. His claws were kneading my shoulder. I couldn't help but shed a tear. "Come on, let's go home."

I gave him a quick kiss on the head without fearing that my lips would get bitten off and he happily went into the carrier without a fuss. If they hadn't checked his microchip information, I could have sworn this wasn't my cat.

I found Zack and Gale chatting in the reception area. They turned towards me when I walked through the door. Gale seemed to look me up and down for signs of scratches, bites and heavy bleeding but all I had were patches of white fur on my chest.

"Is everything okay?" she asked. "He didn't bite you?"

"No, everything's fine." I looked down towards the calm cat in the carrier. "He just wants to get home I think."

"Perfect, that's great." She instantly relaxed. "I'll let you both get him home."

"Thank you," I said, surprised to be happy to have Bing back.

Gale smiled. "No problem."

"What do we owe you?" Zack asked. I hadn't thought of that.

Gale looked from him to me and shook her head. "Happy to have you reunited."

Yes, I thought, *a psycho cat off the premises.* But then wondered if he'd reformed.

❧

Zack pulled up outside my house. "Here you are."

"Thank you. I'm so sorry about tonight. As happy as I am to have Bing home and safe, I didn't want our date to be cancelled."

"Don't worry about it, I'm glad you've got him back. Are you free Friday night? We can try again."

"Yes, definitely." I heard Bing mew on the back seat. "I'd invite you in for a coffee but… I'm not sure how that would go down with His Highness."

Zack laughed. "Not a problem, I'll find somewhere for us to go on Friday and will text you with a time that I'll pick you up."

I was so relieved that he hadn't been put off by the night's drama. It was certainly a story to tell the grandkids. If that was where we ended up of course. Our next date would be more successful. It couldn't go any worse, could it?

CHAPTER 36

$\mathcal{I}$ woke up the next morning to an odd sensation. One I wasn't used to. In all my years of being a cat mum, this had never happened before. I was scared to move at first, not wanting to disturb him. I managed to lift my head enough to look at my new fluffy pillow tucked up between my arm and my body. His fur was tickling the skin under my arm.

When I'd come upstairs to bed, he was at my feet the whole time, but not in a way that suggested he wanted to kill me, for the first time ever. Even when I went to the bathroom, he was super close to me, which proves that cats have no boundaries. When I'd climbed into bed, he got comfy on top of the duvet in between my knees, but sometime during the night he had managed to sneak under the cover and nest himself as close to me as possible.

I carefully reached for my phone with my free hand. I had to take a photo, this had #catselfie written all over it. I just needed to make sure I didn't... bang. The phone slipped from my poor left-handed grip and landed back on the bedside table, but Bing didn't budge. I had to check he was breathing, which he was, luckily. He was in such a deep sleep.

At my second attempt, I managed to pick up my phone and

swipe open the camera. I didn't care that I had some serious bed head going on, this was an amazing photo opportunity. However, once I saw the photo, I decided that people didn't need to see my face after all. Seeing my arm was good enough for this.

I snapped a picture and uploaded it to Facebook and Instagram with the caption "Look who is finally home and giving me some morning loving. Missed my little man – #catselfie #catcuddle #catsofinsta". It's all about the hashtags these days.

Bing took in a deep breath and stretched all his paws out in front of him. I saw his sharp claws digging into the bed, but I didn't tell him off. Not when I saw that one of them had snapped off. Poor guy. He must have been traumatised by something to be this close to me. What happened to him? I'd still like to know how he managed to get all the way to Huddersfield on his own.

I moved my fingers which were in front of his face and his eyes opened, watching them closely. With an almighty jump, he launched himself forward so his head was pushing into my hand for me to stroke him. He half stood and fully faced me, rubbing his head all over my hand.

"Good morning, did you sleep okay?"

I took his stance of front end down, back end up in the air and tail upright as a good sign.

"Shall we get up?" It was a little after eight and I needed a cup of tea.

As I motioned that I was getting up, he jumped down on the floor but didn't run to the door. He stood by the bed, tail up in the air and looked back to make sure I was going to follow him. He wouldn't take a step forward without me.

"I'm coming," I reassured him as I swung my legs out of bed and put my feet next to him. "Come on then. Bathroom first."

Once he had demonstrated how close a cat can get to a human on the toilet without sitting on it himself, we made our way downstairs in unison and into the kitchen.

We walked past his food bowl. There were still biscuits

covering the floor around it from when I got him home the previous night. He didn't seem to know what to do with himself when he first came out of his carrier. I'd put fresh biscuits in his bowl and cold water in the dish next to it. He went straight to the food and took a mouthful while looking around the kitchen as though making sure he was in the right house. Crumbs went everywhere as he struggled to contain them while mewing at the same time. Some had made their way into the water bowl and were swollen and floating on top.

"Shall we get some fresh water?" I asked him as I reached down to pick up the dish. I tipped out the water and let the soggy biscuits get forced down the drain and filled it up with fresh water. As I placed it back down beside the food, he was helping himself to his biscuits. The ones on the floor had already been eaten. He had to be starving, although he didn't look skinny. Clearly I serve the best cat food in Yorkshire.

I flipped on the kettle and realised I'd left my phone upstairs in bed.

"I'll be back in a second, Bing. Hang on."

He didn't hear me, so I snuck out while he was indulging in Purina's finest.

Walking into my bedroom, the sound of squeaking panicked me. Had I stood on a mouse? What the hell was that?

I happened to glance to the landing and saw Bing hurtling up the stairs looking for me. He was all fluffed up and his tail resembled a feather duster. He stopped when he was in between my legs.

"Hey, what's the matter? I only came upstairs."

Mew. Mew. Mew.

"Come on, you silly sausage." I reached my hand down towards his head and he jumped up to meet it and a half-eaten biscuit dropped out of his mouth. "I'm only getting my phone."

I wondered if I should ring the vet. It was as though he was suffering from post-traumatic stress. I'd give them a call.

They didn't open until half past eight, so I left a voicemail for a vet to call me back. They knew all about Bing being missing so hopefully they'd call me straight away.

"Let's go back downstairs, you can finish your food while I have a tea."

My phone rang not long after half eight and it was Dr Judge. I filled him in on Bing's adventures and his current strange mood.

"He's certainly acting out of character, but I wouldn't worry just yet. Let him settle back in at home. He's obviously glad to be back and he seems to have missed you." Dr Judge seemed as shocked as I was. "Give him a couple of days. If you're still worried on Monday, give us a call and I'll make sure he's seen first thing. Make sure he has plenty of water, don't overfeed him though. Give him what he usually has and try to keep him indoors for now. Check him over if you can. If you notice any fleas, ticks or injuries then we'll see him straight away but I don't want to cause him any more stress by bringing him in now."

"That's fine, I'll stay in with him today and see how he does over the weekend. Thank you for calling me back."

I was sitting on the couch with my tea in my phone free hand and Bing had made himself comfy on my lap.

"We'll stay in today, okay? Just us. We can have a lazy day."

And we did.

CHAPTER 37

*O*ur lazy day went by very quickly. I forgot how much I loved daytime telly. The always-fabulously-dressed Lorraine Kelly was followed by Phil and Holly doing their thing, their chemistry almost radiating through my TV and into my living room. No wonder they always won the Daytime TV awards. Their chemistry was surely envied by every married couple in the world.

The *Loose Women* panel looked like they'd prefer to be broadcasting after the watershed so they could say what they really wanted to say about the day's headlines. The lunchtime news was an excuse to get up and make a tuna toastie which Bing was happy to share with me. David Dickinson still looked like he spent too much time on a sunbed hosting his antiques show.

When did Warwick Davis start hosting a game show? Tenable? What does that even mean?

Tipping Point, I'd be amazing at this game. I always made a profit on the 2p machines at Seahouses in Northumberland. My brother used to get so angry when he lost all his money and I was winning all the crappy prizes. I struggled to enjoy The Chase.

The chasers are a little too obnoxious for my liking. I know it's their job, but still.

I should ring Sarah. I couldn't believe she hadn't been pestering me for information on mine and Zack's date. The one date that should have made national news and she hadn't been ringing or texting me. She couldn't be that busy, surely.

I rang, but there was no answer, so I sent her a message.

> Hey! Where are you at? Are you okay? I had the most eventful night EVER! Ring me! Xx

That should get her attention without fail. My phone would be buzzing any minute.

An hour later I sent her another message.

> Hey, what's going on? Where are you? I need to tell you about last night!

By nine that night…

> Have you lost your phone or have your fingers fallen off and that's why you can't reply? I'm getting worried. I'm going to call Max Xx

Suddenly, my phone buzzed and I had a message.

> Hey, sorry! Really busy. Will talk later x

Something was going on with her. She seemed really off before my date with Zack and now she didn't want to hear any potentially juicy gossip. For all she knew, Zack and I could have been up all night having wild passionate sex and we were now in hospital from falling off the bed when trying and failing to perform a weird and wonderful karma sutra position.

> Okay, call me when you can. I'm here if you need me Xx

I didn't want to bother her if she didn't want to talk to me. I know she was really worried about the move to Canada and doing as much wedding planning as she could before she left. When we were doing our final exams at university, I didn't see her for a week because she was so worried about them. Once they were out of the way, she was back to her crazy self, buying us Jägermeister and Tequila shots.

I didn't even look at my phone when it rang, it had to be Sarah.

"Hello?"

"She answers! A miracle."

"Mum." This is why one should always check their phone before answering it. "I'm just in the middle of something."

"At this time of night? Well, I'll make this quick. What are you doing tomorrow? Answer quickly please, no delays so you have time to make something up."

"Oh, erm, well, I erm…" I was never any good when put on the spot.

"Are you at work?"

"No, actually, I've taken the week off…" Why would I admit this? I could have said I was in a meeting.

"Perfect. I'll come over tomorrow at twelve. You can put on a lunch if you like. Goodbye."

And she was gone before I could protest. I couldn't even break the wonderful news that Bing had returned. She wouldn't want to come over if she'd known he was here. Ah well, that'll be a lovely surprise for her.

My phone buzzed again. This time, it was someone who *wanted* to speak to me and even be pleasant in the process.

Hey you, Zack's message began, making my cheeks stretch into a big cheesy grin. *How's the kitty doing? Is he all right? I've managed to rebook our table at Verona's for tomorrow night. It's not until quarter to nine as it's last minute, but we can go for a drink before. I'll pick you up in a taxi at half seven. How does that sound? x*

> That sounds perfect, I'll lock Bing in the house
> so he can't interrupt our night again :) He's not
> left my side all day but seems to be relaxing now.
> Thank you for taking me to pick him up X

> Not a problem, I didn't want you driving to
> Hudds on your own on an evening. And it was
> nice to meet the other man in your life. I hope he
> likes me x

> I'll need to introduce you properly. Maybe soon
> while he's in a loving mood X

I attached the photo of Bing snuggled up to me in bed and sent it to Zack.

> I've never been jealous of a cat until now :p I'll
> speak to you tomorrow x

I managed to giggle out loud which woke up Bing who was nestled on my feet on the couch. His mouth stretched into a yawn and his left paw reached forward at the same time, tickling my knee.

When he relaxed again, he stared at me, blinking his eyes slowly in unison with mine. He'd never looked so happy to be in my company. Maybe this would change our relationship forever. My luck with men was finally on the up.

CHAPTER 38

*I*t was like my mother knew that coming over midday would make things really awkward for me. With this being my second attempt at a date with Zack, I could have done with a day of pampering and relaxing, not cleaning and wondering what to feed her to try and get a little bit of approval. Although with Bing's lack of presence the last few weeks, the house was lacking in white hair, so at least she couldn't pick on me for that.

I had an early trip to Tesco for supplies, and then spent the morning tidying up and preparing a light lunch. I didn't want to eat too much if I was eating out later. I wouldn't tell my mum that though. She doesn't need to know I'm going on a date. She'd want to know who, where, when. Not to mention she doesn't even know who Zack is so I wouldn't put it past her to book a seat at the next table just to get a good look at him.

Bing sought refuge on the top of the couch as I hoovered and did a quick dust around. His ears flickered and his pupils dilated as he looked towards the window as someone made their way down the drive.

"Is she here, Bing?" His face relaxed as I tickled his head. "Come on then, best get this over with."

Bing didn't follow me to the door.

"Good to see you've finally dropped the weight," she stepped into the house as I opened the front door and we leaned in for our very traditional and formal greeting of a kiss on each cheek. "It suits you."

"It's nice to see you too, you can go into the room."

"Lounge, dear. Call it a lounge. A room can mean anywhere."

This is true. I could have sent her down to the damp cellar. Would I do that…

I closed the door as she made her way to the lounge.

"Oh, it's back." She said from the doorway.

"It? You mean Bing, my cat? Yes, he came back yesterday. You must be so relieved, you know how upset I was that he'd been missing, right?"

"Yes, of course, yes. We were all worried about him and hoping he'd be back soon."

I joined her at the door and Bing was glaring at her. "Go sit down, I'll bring in lunch. Would you like a tea or something stronger?"

"Tea, darling, just a tea, thank you."

I'd pulled down the fancy pants teapot from the top cupboard. She always complained that making it directly in the cup wasn't proper so at least I was eliminating one criticism. I needed to stay positive and happy before tonight. I couldn't meet Zack with frown lines in my forehead.

I brought the tea in on a tray and set it on the coffee table, and then brought in another tray with two plates of grilled chicken and salad. There was also a selection of condiments on the side. I pulled the coffee table across to the couch so we could reach.

"Well, this all looks very… lovely." She was surprised. "The last time you made lunch for me it was chicken dippers and potato wedges."

"At least they were Birdseye chicken dippers, not store brand. Only the best here, Mum."

She tutted and pulled a plate towards her, opting for the Salad Cream. It was store brand, she must be lowering her standards.

"So, what's new?" I asked as I grabbed my own plate and sat it in front of me. I figured this lunch choice was the least risky option. Filling enough for the middle of the day but wouldn't leave me feeling bloated later. If I ate slowly enough, I wouldn't risk indigestion either.

"Nothing is new. You know about your brother and the baby. Oh," she put her knife and fork down. "Pat died."

"Who?"

"Pat. You know Pat."

"No, I don't know a Pat. Unless you mean the postman." I smiled.

"We had a postman called Pat too? I never realised it was such a common name. No, Pat, you remember your old teacher Mr Young? Pat was his wife's brother."

"How on earth would I have known my teacher's wife's brother?"

"Well, he was such a lovely chap. Married a woman from India. She had beautiful hair. Always glossy. They had seven children you know."

"Oh yeah?" I knew where this was leading.

"Five girls and two boys. They're about your age. One of the sons is married. He owns a chain of pharmacies. Can't remember his name, but the other son, Zain, he's a doctor and just moved into general practice. And he's single..."

"Nope."

"What do you mean? I'm just updating you on the people in our lives."

"They aren't even in our lives, and I know what you're building up to. And the answer is no."

"But he'd be perfect, a doctor!"

"Mum, if Zain's dad has literally just died, do you really think he would be interested in a blind date right now?"

"Hmm," she wondered. "Well, we can wait a few weeks can't we." She scrunched up her nose in disgust. "Have you got another one of those reed diffusers? I can almost taste it."

❧

After a relatively unpainful but also not pleasant lunch, my mum took her leave and I was then free to consider my outfit for tonight. I was gutted my dress couldn't reach its potential the previous date. I ended up really liking it. I'll have to save it for another occasion. I'm sure as soon as my mum has arranged Pat's son's wedding I could wear it to that.

I quickly showered and stood wrapped in a towel in my bedroom wondering what I could wear. I saw the harem trousers I'd bought on Monday on a whim and decided to try them out with a vest top and I was surprised to see it looked really good. I found a necklace which suited it perfectly too.

There was no make-up drama this time. I went straight for what I knew best and it went on exactly as I wanted it straight away. I sent a selfie to Sarah.

Hope this is a good look, eek! Xx

There was no reply, which I expected, but I tried not to dwell on it too much.

No frown lines tonight. And no drama. This evening would be absolutely perfect.

CHAPTER 39

*C*ircle Lounge was quiet for a change when we arrived. All the seats were empty and music was playing through the speakers. The bouncer had opened the door for us and Zack guided me in with his hand on my back. I could almost feel the electricity vibrating through my body as we walked to the bar and stood side by side.

I ordered a dry white wine and he ordered a bottle of Budweiser. I tried to pay but he wouldn't allow it, but I needed to thank him for helping me to rescue Bing on Wednesday. Maybe I could sneakily pay for dinner. I'd need to figure out how I could do it. I could possibly speak to a waitress when he went to the gents, give them my card to hold behind the bar or something. I'd work it out.

We chose the table by the window and finally could pick up from where we left off without any interruptions.

"So how's the kitty since he's been back home?"

"Very odd, he's not seemed right at all."

"Oh?" Zack looked concerned. "Have you taken him to the vet? I thought you said he was being really loving and affectionate?"

"Yes, that's what I mean. It's odd."

Zack laughed. "Is it *that* out of character for him?"

"Yes, very. He can be such a wanker. I used to think he was trying to kill me the way he'd carry on."

"I had a cat like that." Zack took a swig of his beer and I got a good view of his hands. They were so big and manly. *Focus, Jenny, focus now.* "When I was younger, my mum had this ginger Tom cat. He was nasty. Hissed at me all the time. Used to terrify me. I had to sleep in the garden one night because he wouldn't let me get close to the door to knock for help."

"Aw no." I was imagining a child version of Zack being scared by a big nasty cat and being kept out of his house! I felt really sad for him. Imagine, a small child being kept out of his own bed. Was it too soon in our relationship to climb on his lap and cuddle him? The urge to hump him might take over so, actually, yes it was far too soon. "How old were you?" I took a sip of wine.

"Twenty-two."

The wine I sipped was then, accidentally, spat back into the glass and I laughed a little too loudly.

"What's so funny? He was a bully!"

"I'm sorry." I couldn't stop giggling. "I had visions of you as a small child being traumatised by a vicious tiger, not an adult and a little cat."

Zack tried to hide his smile behind his bottle of Bud. "It was really scary, you know, I feared for my life on a daily basis."

"Why didn't your mum help you?"

"She didn't believe me! Whenever she was around he was all Mr Nice Cat. Rubbed against my legs. Curled up on my lap. Then when she was gone, even if she left the room, oh the little git made my life hell."

"I can sympathise. My relationship with Bing has been rocky to say the least. But yesterday, something changed. I wonder if he'll go back to the old ways. I hope he doesn't."

"What's the worst thing he's ever done to you?"

I tapped my nails against my glass while I thought about my answer. There'd been so many things, it was hard to think of what the worst was. The mouse in the toilet? The spider corpses left around the house? Pooping on my pillow?

"I've now got OCD where I have to kick my shoes before I put them on because I never know if he's left a half-dead, half-alive, half-eaten creature in them for me to find. Which I have done on many occasions. Even if I'm at someone else's house, I can't put my shoes back on without giving them a little nudge out of habit."

"You see, people don't realise, but cats are too intelligent to be domestic pets. They should have their own planet."

"No, they shouldn't. They'd wipe us out before we could destroy all the catnip."

"You have a great sense of humour, you know," he said as I tried not to blush at the sudden compliment. "And your laugh. I love hearing it when I get to your office. I always know I'm going to have a great day if you're there."

My cheeks felt warm. "I can't deny, my day usually perks up when you're there too."

We talked, we laughed, we flirted, and we got to know each other for what felt like hours. In fact, we almost missed our reservation at Verona's so had to make a quick dash out of the door. It was only a two-minute walk across town, but when Zack grabbed hold of my hand and squeezed it tight, I would gladly have walked around with him all night. *Forget the food, this is what I wanted.*

"Is that your phone?"

"Hmm?" I was in a handholding daze.

"Your phone, it's ringing. Don't tell me Bing's run away again? I don't think we'd be allowed back to Verona's if we cancel a second time."

I'd happily go to Burger King with you and bump into the lovely

Rob if that was the only place I could spend time with you. Hang on, he's right. My phone's ringing.

"It's my friend Sarah." Typical that she wanted to talk to me then. "Give me two minutes, I won't be long. Sorry, nothing's going to ruin tonight. I promise." I swiped to answer her horrible, bad timing, owes me a HUGE apology, phone call. "Hello?"

I'm not sure what the noise was that came through the phone, but I'm pretty sure it was not human.

"Sarah? What's going on?"

I could barely make out a few words between the wailing and crying.

"Max... wanker... left me... bastard... slag whore... fucking prick."

"Woah, woah, calm down!"

Zack could hear her cries as I had to move the phone away from my ear and had a look of panic on his face. We stopped walking as we were in view of the restaurant.

"Sarah, what's going on? Talk to me."

"I can't... he's... wedding off. I need you."

I looked up at Zack with regretful eyes. I didn't know what to say. It turned out, I didn't need to say anything. He nodded at me.

"I'm on my way." I threw my phone back in my bag. For fuck's sake.

"Come on, we'll get you in a taxi." He looked so disappointed.

"I'm so, so, so, so, sorry." I can't believe this was happening again. I felt like I wasn't destined to have the man of my dreams. *He'll go off me now. He won't want to even attempt to see me again.* What man would?

"Your friend seemed really upset, what going on?"

"I don't know, but it doesn't sound good. Not good at all. I'm really sorry. I hate that this has happened again!"

"Listen, it's okay. Shit happens."

He seemed annoyed. This was our last date, I could tell.

We arrived at the taxi rank, one located next door to a Dixy

Chicken which was very convenient after a night of heavy drinking, and he ordered me a taxi through the little window.

"Silver car," said the operator. When I looked at the five silver taxi's waiting in front of me, he eventually got off his backside to point to the Nissan on the end.

We walked to the car and I turned to Zack to say goodbye, probably forever. I wanted to cry.

Zack suddenly put both of his hands on my face and pulled me in for a kiss. An amazing kiss. A tingle-tastic, tongue-twisting kiss. The best kiss I have ever had in my life. It was so unexpected. Is this a "goodbye forever" kiss? A "this is what you could have had" kiss? I can't believe how good this kiss is, it was just like my dreams.

"I planned on doing that at the end of our date," he said as he pulled away from my lips, his face still close to mine. "If this is where our date is ending then I had to do it now." He was smiling. This was a good sign, right?

"I'm glad you did, I was worried you'd go off me for ditching you again."

"Your friend sounded like she needed you, and quickly. You tell me when you're free and we will try again."

"Third time lucky?"

"Absolutely. I'll be counting it as our third date too, by the way." He leaned in for another kiss which was interrupted by the taxi driver coughing. "Go on, get going. Text me tomorrow."

"Will do." I cheekily pulled him in for another sneaky kiss before climbing into the taxi. "I'll speak to you tomorrow."

He closed the door for me and gave a little wave before heading back to the window to order his taxi too. Thinking back to the call from Sarah, it didn't sound good at all. What was I going to find when I got to her house?

CHAPTER 40

$\mathcal{I}$ arrived at Sarah's house quite quickly. These taxi drivers don't mess about. Especially on a Friday night when they would be getting a lot of business. It was a race to get back to the taxi rank for the next fare. Normally I'd comment about them doing twice the speed limit, but I needed to get to my friend as soon as possible. If I just kept my head down and didn't see what was happening, then it wasn't really happening.

I found her in a heap on the kitchen floor, surrounded by used tissues. Her hair was matted in, what looked like, a combination of tears and snot. Her bloodshot eyes looked up at me. We've both been in some states, but I'd never seen her like this. Not ever. I could only remember ever seeing her cry once. We went to Leeds Fest when we were twenty but lost each other in the crowds. When we eventually found each other, in our drunken states, it was a very emotional reunion.

"Sarah! What the hell's happened?" I ran towards her and sat down and she collapsed into me.

"He's gone," she managed to say. "We're over."

"What do you mean? You can't be over."

She pulled the last of the tissues from the box and blew her nose. I had an urge to get her a glass of water. All that crying must have made her dehydrated. My mother would be so proud of my maternal instinct. I stood up and went to the cupboard.

"He's been seeing someone else."

The words hit me like a thump to the chest This couldn't be true. Max would never do that. I almost dropped the glass I'd pulled out of the cupboard.

"He... he what?"

"Yep." She wiped her nose. "The wanker's been shagging someone else."

"How could he *do* that to you?"

"He said he hasn't been happy for a while. 'A long time', he said. Apparently, that's the only reason he proposed. He thought it would make things better for us to have something to look forward to, but he still wasn't happy. And that's when he met Ellie. Such a tramp name. *Ellie*. Smelly Ellie, tramp-whore Ellie."

I handed Sarah the glass of water and was glad that she drank some. I didn't know how long she'd been crying but there were red streaks down each of her cheeks from the tears and not an ounce of make-up left on her face.

"And he told you all this tonight?"

"No. Oh, no. He didn't tell me." She got up off the floor and put the glass on the kitchen counter. "Why be honest and walk away from the woman who has loved you all this time when you can cheat on her and make a fool of her."

"So how do you know all this?"

"In my drunken state last Saturday, when I got home after our night out." She took a deep breath. "I put some leftover lasagne in the microwave to have before bed. I was so hungry. Some of his bank statements were on top of it and I'd accidentally knocked them on the floor. I picked them up and thought I'd put them away in his files when I noticed the transactions. I saw a lot of outgoings, so I had a nosy at what they were and there were payments for meals out, hotel rooms, on nights that he was supposedly working away."

"Wouldn't he be staying at hotels?" I said as I saw bank statements strewn all over the kitchen table. Some were torn in pieces.

"Yes, but the company pays for those. He has a company credit card. And they were expensive meals for only one person. Anyway, I got a little paranoid so went on his iPad and logged on to his Facebook."

"What did you find?"

It was when Sarah turned to face me that I noticed how thin she was and how tired she looked. She mustn't have eaten or slept for nearly a week.

"Messages. Photos. Disgusting photos. Plans and arrangements. Details of… how great the sex was between them. How neither of them had ever had it so good." How Sarah had any tears left, I didn't know. But her eyes soon filled up again.

"And you've known this all week? Why didn't you tell me?" This explained why she seemed off with me, and instantly replied when I threatened to call Max.

"I… I didn't want to accept it was true. I don't get it, why would he? We were moving to Canada, I was quitting my job, my life, my home, all my family and friends, why would he let me do all that?"

I pulled her close to me and hugged her tightly while she cried into my shoulder. Like we did at Leeds Fest, but this time we weren't slow dancing to the music in the background while declaring how much we loved each other and would never lose each other again.

"So, what did you do?"

"I was too scared to say anything. But tonight… he said he had to go away on Monday for a few days for work. And I knew it was a lie. So, I confronted him. I snapped. I had to say something."

"What *did* you say?"

"I said I know about Ellie. That's it. 'I know about Ellie'. And he just stood there. Like a deer in the headlights. I thought he'd cry. Panic. Apologise. Be a little remorseful. Anything. He said, 'I'm leaving you.'"

"He didn't say sorry?"

"No. The bastard. Totally in the wrong and then makes out like he just decided to leave me now because he's fallen in love with someone else."

"Woah, what? In love?"

"Yep. They're in love. He's at her house. Had the nerve to call her while he was upstairs packing."

"Is he like, having an early midlife crisis or something?"

I didn't understand. Max was the good guy. This was never supposed to happen. They would be starting a new life in a new country and getting married. They were the couple that everyone wanted to be. Everyone envied their life together.

"I don't know." She held her hand to her mouth and shook her head. "I don't know what I did wrong."

"Hey, you did *nothing* wrong."

"I must have done *something* wrong. Or not done something to keep him happy. Why else would he be looking elsewhere?"

"Because he's a wanker. He doesn't deserve you. He'll realise what he's done in time, the huge mistake he's made, but by then it'll be too late."

"What do I do *now*?"

"You go and wash your face then sit down and rest. I'll crack open a bottle."

"Okay." She picked up the kitchen roll and tore off a couple of sheets to blow her nose and wipe her eyes, it was then that she looked at me properly. "Wait, why are you so dressed up?"

"Erm, I was out. Nothing important."

"But you look so... oh shit. Jenny. Shit. I'm so sorry." She looked mortified. "Oh my God, I can't believe it. You were with Zack, weren't you?"

"Yes, but don't worry! Don't think about it. I can tell you about that later."

"You shouldn't have come. I shouldn't have called you. I'm such a selfish cow."

"Yes, you should call me. Sistas before Mistas. He understands, and we can rearrange. It's fine. Go sort yourself out and I'll find the good wine."

"Text him. Rearrange something. I'll feel better if I know you've got another date lined up with him. Please."

"Okay, I'll text him." I found my bag by the door where I'd dropped it when I walked in and pulled out my phone. "I'll text him now, but you go upstairs and freshen up. Go."

She finally obeyed and went upstairs. When I looked at my phone, I already had a message waiting for me.

I hope your friend is okay x

> She's in a bit of a state but she'll live. Think I'll stay here with her tonight. Are you free tomorrow for the 'third' date? X

I can be free, it depends how tempting the offer is ;) X

> How about dinner at mine? I'll cook and show off my culinary delights. Phone will be switched off! X

That is a tempting offer. How can I refuse? Let me know what time you want me x

Want you? I've wanted you for years.

> How's seven? X

I'll be there x

&

Sarah and I ordered a Chinese feast, which was her choice. I'd not had one for a long time, not since fart-gate with Dan. I'd forgotten how good it was. The spring rolls had the right amount of crunch on the outside and moistness on the inside. I was glad we bought a portion each. We ate everything. Sarah looked like she hadn't eaten properly all week. She *certainly* made up for it. We both did.

We talked late into the night about Max. I honestly couldn't believe what he'd done. It goes to show that you never really know someone, or what goes on behind closed doors. What seems like a perfect relationship could in fact be a disaster waiting to happen. In a way, it was good she found out before the wedding, and the move, but how long would he allow it to go on for? Until they landed in Canada?

Sarah decided not to call her parents until the next day. She knew her mum would want all the information and would want to come over and make a fuss, and her dad would be shouting in the background that he was going to kill Max for treating his little girl like this. She couldn't face it yet but knew they would help with cancelling any wedding plans.

"I don't even want to get into our bed," she said. "He could have shagged her up there for all I know."

"I'll sleep in there, you take the single in the spare room."

I suddenly felt a gurgle in my tummy. I might have eaten too much. I wasn't used to big greasy feasts anymore and my stomach was reminding me of that. At least I'd be sleeping alone.

"Would you mind?"

"Not at all. I'm pretty tired now though."

And I wasn't surprised. It was almost 2am.

"We can call it a night. I'll try to face it all again in the morning. Maybe I'll wake up and it'll have been a dream, a nightmare."

I felt so sorry for her. She'd had it all mapped out. The home, the marriage, the move. Sarah wanted three children. Any sons would be on the local football teams and daughters would be dancers. Their home was the perfect size for a big family, which was why Sarah worked so bloody hard to be able to afford it. And now she faced losing her dream home because the love of her life couldn't keep it in his pants. She would be single. Just as I was on the verge of getting my own dream man.

Sarah went to pick up our plates which had been left on the floor along with the food cartons.

"Leave all that, we'll do it in the morning." There was no point in cleaning up. It was only us two.

We walked upstairs and said our goodnights, and I gave her one last hug.

"You're going to be fine," I reassured her. "It's going to get worse before it gets better, but it *will* get better. I promise you. Everything will be sorted out. The wedding, the house, minor details that are easy to fix."

Sarah and Max's bed was amazeballs. It was a memory foam mattress. Once I sunk into it, I knew I wouldn't be moving all night. If she decided to get rid of it, and Max didn't take it to wherever his new love nest was, I wonder if it'd be rude to see if I could have it.

Pop.

What was that?

Pop.

Oh Christ, not again. What was it about Chinese takeaways that did this to me? At least I was alone this time. No one there to witness my trumping trauma.

Pop.

CHAPTER 41

I woke up in the exact same position I had fallen asleep in. This bed was seriously amazing. Dan could do with trying it out and getting rid of that waterbed disaster he thought was such a good idea. I sat up and had an urge to fart. How there was any gas left after the previous night I don't know. There was a pain shooting through my tummy though. I had to let it out. I rolled onto Max's side of the bed to do it. It was the least he deserved.

I checked my phone and it had just turned nine. Sarah would still be in bed. I bet she needed a good night sleep. All that wine, food and talking should have helped. I slipped my clothes back on and crept out to the landing trying and failing not to walk on the creaky floorboards. The door to the spare room was open. When I nipped in to see if she was okay, I saw the bed was empty.

When I got downstairs, I saw that Sarah had been very busy. The living room had been tidied of our mess from last night and she was in the kitchen giving it a good clean.

"Morning," I said as I walked in. The dishwasher was rumbling in the corner and the smell of kitchen cleaner was thick in the air.

"Hey, did you sleep okay?" she asked as soon as she saw me.

"Fine, that is a comfy bed. How are you feeling?"

"I'm okay. I think I'm okay." She dropped the cloth she was using into the sink. "Obviously it's really shit, but I've spoken to my mum already and briefly filled her in. They're coming over later on and I'll tell them properly what happened. They're going to stay over too."

"That's good." I felt guilty that I'd be leaving her but knowing her parents would be there made me feel better. "Have you heard anything from Max at all?"

"Nothing. Fuck him."

"That's the spirit."

She looked at me and the corner of her mouth twitched into a slight smile.

"That's better," I said, "I wondered where you'd gone."

"I'm here. It's such a shock. It doesn't seem real. I thought about it all last night and… I'm single." She twiddled her wedding finger, displaying a white mark where her engagement ring had been. "What do I do now? I wasn't supposed to be single again at this age. It was all meant to be mapped out. I don't know how to be single."

"It's not difficult. Food shopping is less stressful I imagine. But maybe get a dog instead of a cat. Dogs are loyal. Cats will rip you off. That's where I went wrong." I flicked the switch on the kettle and started to make us both a tea. "Seriously though, don't think about that for now. Think about you. You deserve some you time. I'll book us in to the Titanic Spa again if you want. We can make a weekend of it. And we can head to York for a day out. We can do anything you want. The world is your oyster."

"Maybe… maybe we could do that girls' holiday we have been talking about for years. We always say we needed a girly holiday abroad but never got around to it because of life getting in the way. Maybe now is the time?"

"You read my mind. What do you think to Rome?"

"Sounds perfect." She smiled. "We're not sharing a room though. Not after what I heard last night through the wall. You might want to get some Imodium before your big date tonight." She winked at me.

For God's sake. I'm NEVER getting a Chinese again.

🦢

Sarah offered to drive me home, but I needed to call at Tesco which wasn't far from hers, so I walked on and said I would get a taxi home from there. I left at eleven so I'd have time to hunt around the aisles for tonight's tea with Zack.

I told Sarah that I had planned on making fajitas for Zack, my new favourite meal. It's fairly easy to make but so good. I always put some mayonnaise and lettuce in the wrap first, and then fill it with spicy chicken. Plus, a side of guacamole to dip it in. You can't go wrong with fajitas. Until Sarah told me that it's a very messy meal to eat with a guy you fancy. She had a point. No matter how much I wrap them up, the juice from the sauce mixed with the mayonnaise always drips out of the bottom. I'm not ashamed to admit that I lick it off my fingers, but I have to sit with sheets of kitchen roll on my lap every time. That wouldn't look very attractive.

"You can still do spicy chicken," Sarah had said. *"Put it on a plate with some salad and maybe some new potatoes or something. Forget the wraps."*

I like that idea, but not the new potatoes. I don't want Zack thinking I'm a crazy healthy person. We can't kick off a potential new relationship with a lie. I need something on the side but what can it be? Chips. Couldn't go wrong with chips.

The taxi dropped me off home just after twelve. I'm pleased to report that he was a sensible driver who followed the speed limit, mostly. I walked through the gate and my heart melted at what I saw in the window.

Bing was sat up on his bum, front paws up on the glass, and he was meowing at me. I hadn't planned on being away from him the previous night. I felt so guilty!

"Hey, little man!" I walked through the door and he ran straight to my legs, rubbing all over them and covering me in white hair.

Mew! Mew!

"I'm here. Did you miss me? Or do you just need food?"

He'd probably just want food. He followed me into the kitchen. There was plenty of food in his bowl, and his water was fine too. Did he miss me after all? Bless him. He was like a whole new cat.

"Right, Bing. We have a big job. We need to marinate this chicken to get it ready for tonight. Have a big, big, big clean up. And you," I knelt down on the floor and he jumped up on my leg. "You're meeting someone very special tonight. I need you to be a good boy. Can you be a good boy?"

He rubbed his head against my chin. I had no doubts that he'd be a good boy for me. In fact… I think I love this cat.

CHAPTER 42

I watched Zack walk down the garden from the living room window, standing far enough back in the room so he couldn't see me glaring at him like a nosy neighbour watching your every move. When he knocked on the door, I decided I should count to five before going to open it so I didn't seem too eager to have him in the house. My house. With me. On a date with me in my house. Eek!

He looked even yummier than ever. At work, he always looked smart. On our two dates, he looked suave. That night, he looked sexually casual. He was wearing dark blue jeans and a black shirt. The top two buttons were undone, the sleeves rolled up to his elbows and in one hand he was carrying a bottle of wine.

Knock knock.

One Mississippi. Two Mississippi. Three Mississippi.

(The longest five seconds ever)

Four Mississippi.

Deep breath.

Five Mississippi.

It was the third time we'd seen each other out of work, why was I so nervous? The food was going to be fantastic. I'd cooked it so many times, it couldn't go wrong. I was wearing my blue summery dress and my legs were still good from my last wax. The old bikini line was presentable too, just in case. I also might have been wearing my new matching bra and knicker set from Boux Avenue. It was always best to be prepared. Plus, the bra gave me some good cleavage.

I took a deep breath before I reached for the handle. I heard Bing's paws padding down the hallway. When I glanced behind me, he was making his way into the living room. No doubt to have a nosy out the window at who our visitor was. What did I say about nosy neighbours?

I opened the door. "Hello." I smiled and Zack smiled back, but it was a nervous smile. Why would he be nervous?

"Hi, wow, you look amazing."

"Thank you." I blushed. "Come in."

He walked into the hallway and stood behind me as I closed the door, putting the lock on. I realised this might seem like I was locking him in as my prisoner (if only) but it was a habit from living alone all this time.

I turned to face him, feeling the heat rising in my cheeks and my heart going crazy. His eyes slipped down to look at my lips and he leaned in. As his lips touched mine, my legs almost lost their balance. I put my hand on his chest to steady myself and I could feel his heart beating hard too.

He was such a good kisser. I could kiss him forever.

Something startled him, and he pulled away.

"Ahh, what was that?" He looked down at his legs.

Bing had decided to come and say hello by jumping up and putting his front paws onto Zack's legs. Bing's tail was waving as his whiskers stretched forward showing how curious he was to meet him.

"It looks like Bing wants to meet you properly. He didn't get much of a chance when you helped me get him from the vets."

"Hello, Bing." Zack knelt down and held out his hand which was exactly what Bing wanted. All I could think was "please don't bite him, please don't damage those beautiful hands that I hope to have all over me at some point". Bing sniffed and licked and rubbed his head in to his palm. "It's nice to finally meet you."

It was rare to see Bing be nice to anyone other than Sarah.

"Would you like a drink?" I asked Zack.

"Oh here, I brought you a bottle of wine." He stood, leaving Bing wanting more. I knew that feeling. Zack handed me the bottle of wine in his hand. "I know you like white."

"Thank you that's really kind. I got you some bottles of Bud if you want that instead?"

"Great, thanks."

"It's in the kitchen, come on through." He followed me to the kitchen where the food was all prepped and the table was set. "Do you like fajitas?"

"I love fajitas."

"Well, it's kind of deconstructed fajitas. No wraps but we have chips."

"You can't go wrong with chips."

*Oh, he is **so** perfect. We're so meant to be.*

I reached into the fridge and got a bottle of Bud. I had a careful job getting them from the aisle of the store to the taxi and into the house. I didn't want them to be too shaken up for when I opened one for him, resulting in my good dress being drenched in beer. Although a good excuse to take off my dress and show off my underwear, I needed a glass of wine before any disasters occurred.

Success. The bottle didn't explode in my hand.

"Here you go." I handed it to him.

"Thank you."

I opened the bottle of wine and poured myself a modest sized glass. I would be taking small sips before I had any food. I needed a level head if I was cooking chicken. We couldn't have our third date being a disaster too because we wound up with food poisoning. I only have one toilet, we couldn't risk it.

We clinked our drinks and toasted an interruption-free evening.

We stood next to each other in the kitchen, not knowing quite what to do with ourselves. We weren't restricted by being out in a bar or restaurant. We weren't in a car on a cat rescue mission. It was just me and him. Alone. No interruptions. Besides the attention-seeking cat, of course, who'd found his new best friend. I should have found a playlist for some background music, but I had no idea what music Zack was into.

"Why don't you see to your new buddy and I'll get started on food?"

"As much as I like him, I'd rather stay and help you cook." He gazed at me in a way that almost made me melt on the spot. "Do you need me to do anything?"

Take me. Lift up my dress and take me now.

"Erm, not really." I had to look away before I combusted so much I could cook the chicken on myself. "It's only the chicken that needs cooking." I smiled at how organised I'd been with very little time to prepare. I'd managed to do the food shop, come back and give the house a thorough clean, prepped the food and then showered and made myself presentable. A dutiful wife in the making. My mother would probably think my domestic goddessness was all down to her but, in all honesty, I had recently started watching *Desperate Housewives* on Amazon Prime and getting my tips from Bree, despite being more of a Susan.

The chips were already in the oven being baked to perfection and the chicken wouldn't take long to cook. I grabbed the Pyrex bowl from the fridge where the chicken had been marinating in olive oil and fajita mix. The spicy smell filled the kitchen once I opened the fridge door.

"Where's the pan?" he asked.

"In that cupboard there." I pointed to the cupboard next to the oven. "The wok will do. Thanks."

He had to bend down to reach to get it so I had a sneaky stare at his bum which looked edible in those jeans. I think he could wear a suit of body armour and make it look sexy.

He placed it on top of the cooker and I appeared next to him with the bowl of chicken and switched on the hob. He didn't move from beside me. It was very off-putting. I was scared I was going to drop the bowl. There couldn't be any disasters though, so I put the chicken straight into the pan. It wasn't hot enough yet, but I was.

I kept my eyes on the chicken. "It's erm... it won't take long to cook."

"Good." I could feel his eyes on me. I had tingles in my neck. Down my spine. Travelling down my legs and into my toes. I didn't know how much longer I could keep this up.

I dared to look at Zack. He was so close to me. The anticipation was quickly building in my body. I was being pulled to him, like a magnet, and he wasn't pulling away. Instead, his hand gripped my waist and he pulled my body against his as we kissed. It was different to when we kissed outside the taxi rank. That was a kiss of reassurance, that we weren't over. This was a kiss to show that we were just beginning, and that the best was yet to come.

I threw my arms around his neck as both of his hands held me and moved around my body. The tingles were out of control. They were sizzling. I could almost hear them. Hang on... that was the chicken. Dammit.

He heard it too.

"Turn it off," he said through heavy breaths.

I did as I was told and turned off the hob and the oven. Food was not important. His hands never left my body.

"Where's your bedroom?" he asked as I faced him again.

"Upstairs."

We were moving. Kissing and moving. Out of the kitchen. Down the hallway. The kissing had to stop at the stairs, but the touching didn't. I led the way up the stairs and he stayed close enough to keep his hands on my waist. As we reached my room, which had also been thoroughly cleaned, I closed the door in case Bing tried to make it a ménage à trois.

Zack found the zip on the back of my dress and slowly pulled it down as I undid the remaining buttons on his shirt. I put my hands on his bare chest as he took his hands off my dress to take his shirt off fully. I opened my eyes to look at him, to take him in. There weren't any faults on his perfect physique. I wanted to lick his chest, but I wasn't sure what he would think to that.

His hands returned to my dress that he could easily slip off now it was undone. He wasn't shy about looking at me. With the pressure I felt pushing against my hip, I could tell that he liked what he saw too. It became even clearer when he slipped his jeans off.

As we fell to the bed, I started to worry. Thinking back over my bad luck with men, I didn't want this to go wrong. It had to be perfect. I was having flashbacks to my rendezvous with James and the last time with Dan. It had all gone so wrong. What if this ended up a disaster too?

Zack's hands moved down my body, followed by his lips which were kissing me all the way to the top of my knickers. I was so glad I checked that my bikini line was looking good. He slipped my knickers down and carried on kissing me, teasing me. I was so turned on, he could touch me with a feather and I would be done.

As he moved his way back up to my face, I realised he'd sneakily slipped off his boxers too. My legs instinctively opened, eagerly awaiting what would come next. *This is it. This is what I've been waiting for, dreaming about, fantasizing about. What if it's no good? What if he's another James?*

That's the thing about moments. They have the ability to surprise you. Have you ever been so excited about something that you couldn't wait for it to happen? The build-up of anticipation and tingles where a single touch would make you explode in a world of pleasure.

This, I'm pleased to say, was one of those moments.

It was pleasure that I'd never felt before. Explosions, fireworks. I'd never had it so good. And it had never repeated for me before, I thought that was a myth. Once on the bottom and then again when we rolled so I could be on top. Fate had been saving this experience for me, so I could have it with my perfect guy. Zack. My Zack.

We laid alongside each other. I was tucked into his nook and he held me tightly. I could smell his sweat mixed with his aftershave which created a whole new kind of aroma that I wanted bottled up. I'm not sure how long we laid with each other, but we were interrupted by the sound of grumbling bellies.

"Hmm," he moved slightly so he could kiss the top of my head, "I think that was my belly."

"I think it was both of our bellies, telling us they want feeding. I think the chicken will be ruined now."

"True, I *am* hungry though."

"I might have something in the freezer we could have." It wouldn't be as exciting as my spicy chicken and chips tea, but anything would do. I was starving. I'd not had much to eat all day because of my nerves putting me off, but having relaxed I could eat anything right now.

I moved closer to him to take in more of his smell. I couldn't stop smiling. Our date had been a success. No interruptions. No problems. It was absolutely perfect. Nothing could go wrong now.

"Is there anything you particularly fancy?" he asked.

"You're the guest, we'll look in the freezer and you can pick something."

"Or we could get a takeaway, less effort. Do you have a good Chinese near here?"

Dammit, so close.

THE END

A NOTE FROM THE PUBLISHER

Thank you for reading this book. If you enjoyed it please do consider leaving a review on Amazon to help others find it too.

We hate typos. All of our books have been rigorously edited and proofread, but sometimes mistakes do slip through. If you have spotted a typo, please do let us know and we can get it amended within hours.

info@bloodhoundbooks.com

Printed in Great Britain
by Amazon

23574856R00126